Detective

Shadows of Dominion

Shadows of Dominion City

Detective Max Carter, Volume 2

Oscar Wayne

Published by Oscar Wayne, 2024.

This is a work of fiction. Similarities to real people, places, or events are entirely coincidental.

SHADOWS OF DOMINION CITY

First edition. November 19, 2024.

Copyright © 2024 Oscar Wayne.

ISBN: 979-8230080602

Written by Oscar Wayne.

Table of Contents

Chapter 1: The Disappearance 1
Chapter 2: Shadows in Power 21
Chapter 3: A Network of Lies 43
Chapter 4: The Cult Unveiled 60
Chapter 5: Another Murder 79
Chapter 6: Descent into Darkness 99
Chapter 7: Finding the Cult 119
Chapter 8: The Rescue Attempt 132
Chapter 9: Exposing the Cult 146
Chapter 10: Dominion's Downfall 160

Chapter 1: The Disappearance

The late afternoon light cast Dominion City in an amber glow, filtering through the dense row of towering buildings that lined the street. People were already streaming out of offices, eager to catch the last moments of the day. Just outside *The Last Sip*, an upscale café frequented by the city's elite, Emily Lawson stepped onto the sidewalk. She clutched a leather-bound file to her side and checked her phone, her face tense with a mixture of determination and apprehension.

Emily had planned this day meticulously, yet every step felt like a risk. She paused a moment to gather herself, her thumb hovering over the screen as she typed a quick message. "I have the file. Headed there now." She hit send, glancing around the nearly empty street, hoping she could pass through unnoticed. With one last look over her shoulder, she began walking, her heels clicking against the pavement.

In her line of vision, a sleek black van appeared, idling a short distance down the street. She paid it no attention at first, lost in thought and focused on her mission, but as she neared, the van's engine rumbled to life, and it slowly pulled up alongside her. Emily's instinct kicked in, but before she could react, the sliding door whipped open. Two figures, faces obscured by dark ski masks, leaped out, closing the space between them in a heartbeat.

"Hey!" Emily barely had time to yell before a gloved hand clamped over her mouth, muffling her scream. She struggled, her legs kicking wildly, but the second figure grabbed her arms, yanking her back toward the open door of the van. Her phone clattered to the ground, the screen still illuminated with her last message, and her bag slipped from her shoulder, its contents spilling across the sidewalk.

Several bystanders emerged from a nearby alley, drawn by the commotion, but by then it was too late. Emily was shoved inside the van, the door slammed shut, and in seconds, the vehicle roared away, leaving a few scattered pieces of evidence behind.

A young man, who had been lingering on the street corner with a coffee cup in hand, hurried over to the scene, his face pale as he recognized the name on the phone's screen. "Oh no... that's Emily Lawson," he muttered, eyes wide with shock. Emily wasn't just anyone in Dominion City; she was the daughter of Senator Robert Lawson, one of the most powerful figures in the city. Within minutes, word began to spread like wildfire. People gathered, speculating, whispering in hushed tones, while others began snapping pictures of the dropped phone and scattered belongings with their phones, eagerly uploading them to social media.

Police sirens soon echoed in the distance, and the crowd parted as officers arrived to cordon off the area. Dominion City was about to be thrown into a frenzy, and Emily Lawson's kidnapping was only the beginning.

Detective Max Carter leaned back in his chair; eyes closed as the hum of Dominion City's police headquarters pulsed around him. Papers piled high on his desk held remnants of cases, mostly robberies, assaults, and other mundane crimes, yet none could erase the shadow that loomed over him from his own past. Today had felt like any other, until his superior, Captain Daniels, had pulled him aside with a look of grim urgency.

Now, in the crowded, buzzing briefing room, Max waited with a sense of foreboding. Around him, officers murmured in low tones, and the tension in the air was unmistakable. Then Captain Daniels stepped forward, his deep voice cutting through the noise.

"As most of you have heard, Emily Lawson, the daughter of Senator Robert Lawson, has been kidnapped." He paused, allowing the weight of his words to settle over the room. "This is high profile. The media's already caught wind, and the senator's office is demanding swift action."

Max's stomach tightened. A high-profile case meant layers of pressure, bureaucracy, and political oversight—a tangled mess that would make solving it that much harder. Still, a disappearance was a case that would pull him from the monotony of minor crimes and, if nothing else, push him toward something worthwhile.

"Carter," Captain Daniels said, nodding at him, "you're lead on this one."

Max met his gaze with a slight nod, his calm exterior masking the storm of thoughts already brewing in his mind. He knew the media frenzy would only intensify with every hour that passed. And the deeper he got, the less chance he'd have for a quiet, objective investigation. He'd have to move quickly, or this case would be swallowed by red tape and rumors.

"Do we have any suspects?" Max asked, his voice steady, masking his apprehension.

Daniels shook his head. "Not yet. Just the preliminary reports from witnesses, but it was swift, clean. They knew what they were doing. We're pulling surveillance footage now."

Just as Max began formulating his first steps, the door swung open, and the last person he wanted to see walked in—Adrian Cross. Slick and confident, Adrian had the kind of smile that could melt a news camera and a self-assured strut that had always grated on Max's nerves. A former partner turned rival, Adrian was as ambitious as they came, often willing to cut corners to be the first to break a case and make headlines.

"Daniels," Adrian said with a nod, ignoring Max completely. "Heard about the case, and I figured you'd want someone who knows the city's power players. My contacts could be of... interest."

Max's jaw clenched, a barely perceptible flicker of annoyance flashing across his face. He knew Adrian's methods—how he reveled in the attention cases like this brought him. To him, every case was a career move, a path to further elevate his reputation and political connections.

"Cross," Daniels replied, "you're on this one, too. I don't have time for your turf war, so keep it professional."

Max felt a rush of irritation, but he kept his expression impassive. Working alongside Adrian was the last thing he wanted. As the others filed out, Max found himself face to face with his rival.

"Well, Carter," Adrian said, his voice dripping with sarcasm, "fancy seeing you on a case this high-profile. I suppose they just handed it to you."

Max shot him a withering look. "This isn't a competition, Cross. You'd do well to remember that."

Adrian chuckled, adjusting the cuffs of his impeccably tailored suit. "Oh, I know. Just be sure to keep up."

The challenge in Adrian's words was clear, and Max felt the familiar frustration rise within him. But he pushed it down, reminding himself that Emily Lawson's life was what mattered. This wasn't about one-upping Adrian. Not yet, anyway.

The next morning, Dominion City University's campus felt subdued, shrouded in an uneasy silence. News of Emily Lawson's kidnapping had swept through the community, and though classes

SHADOWS OF DOMINION CITY

continued, a somber cloud hung over the students and faculty. Max walked through the quad, his eyes scanning faces for any flicker of recognition or guilt. He'd called in a handful of Emily's friends and acquaintances, hoping to find leads—or, at the very least, a sense of who she was.

In the bustling campus café, Max spotted his first interviewee. Leah Brighton sat at a corner table, nervously stirring a half-empty cup of coffee. She glanced up as Max approached, her eyes widening with a mixture of curiosity and fear.

"Leah Brighton?" Max asked, keeping his voice calm as he took a seat across from her. Leah nodded, her hand tightening around her coffee cup.

"Y-yes. I'm sorry, Detective. I just... I can't believe this is happening. Emily's... she's one of my best friends," Leah stammered, her voice quivering.

Max softened his tone. "I understand. I know this is difficult, but anything you can tell me about Emily might help us find her."

Leah took a shaky breath, tucking a strand of hair behind her ear. "Emily... she was always so driven, you know? She wanted to change things, make a difference. I think she took after her father, but... well, recently she's been more secretive."

Max raised an eyebrow. "Secretive how?"

Leah hesitated, glancing around as if someone might overhear. "She'd been... meeting people, people she wouldn't talk about. I think she got involved in something bigger. Sometimes, she'd tell me she was going to 'fix' things, like she was uncovering something."

"What kind of things? Did she ever mention specifics?"

"She wouldn't tell me details," Leah replied, her brow furrowing in thought. "But she seemed... scared. Like she was in over her head. And then, a couple of weeks ago, she stopped mentioning it altogether. I think she knew something bad was going to happen."

Max nodded, his mind churning. Leah's words hinted that Emily may have been onto something significant, perhaps tied to her father's political sphere. But fear and caution might have driven her to silence.

"Thank you, Leah. You've been very helpful," Max said, standing. Leah gave him a sad smile before he moved on to the next name on his list.

Max's next stop was Dominion City's high-rise office district, where he met Jake Morrison, a young man with slicked-back hair and a firm handshake. Jake, Emily's ex-boyfriend, was a recent graduate with aspirations in local politics. He projected confidence, but Max could see the nerves flickering in his eyes.

"Mr. Morrison," Max said as they settled into a conference room in Jake's office building. "Thank you for meeting with me. I understand you and Emily were close."

Jake's jaw clenched. "We were, yeah. She's... important to me, Detective. This whole thing is... I mean, who would do this?"

"That's what I'm trying to find out," Max replied evenly. "I understand you two had an argument recently?"

Jake looked away, his face tense. "We disagreed on some things. It happens. She... she was passionate, you know? Always wanting to dig up trouble, point fingers. Especially with her father's connections, she thought she could get away with it."

Max noted Jake's bitterness. "What kind of trouble was she digging up?"

Jake shifted uncomfortably. "I don't know, honestly. But she wouldn't let things go. Even if it meant ruining her family's name.

She talked about exposing things, but she was always so vague." He scoffed. "Guess it was one of those causes she didn't want me to be a part of."

Max studied him for a long moment, filing away the resentment Jake couldn't hide. "Did you feel Emily's efforts could jeopardize your career?"

Jake's eyes narrowed, a flicker of irritation flashing across his face. "Look, Detective, I had nothing to do with this. We had differences, sure, but I would never hurt her. I wanted her to be safe. And I wouldn't risk my career over something so... so reckless."

Max remained silent, letting the weight of his questions linger. Jake, despite his confident demeanor, seemed uncomfortable and unwilling to share much more. Max thanked him and left, sensing that Jake's ambitions might have clashed with Emily's drive for justice.

The final interview of the morning was with Darren Blake, Senator Lawson's assistant. Darren had a sharp, narrow face, his eyes darting nervously as he met Max in the senator's office building.

"Thank you for agreeing to speak with me," Max began, keeping his tone steady as they sat down in a secluded conference room.

"Of course," Darren replied quickly, adjusting his tie. "Anything to help find Emily. She's... she's practically family."

Max watched him carefully. "You've worked with the senator for several years, haven't you?"

"Yes, almost five," Darren replied, a note of pride in his voice. "I know the Lawsons well."

Max leaned in slightly. "I understand Emily was getting involved in some sensitive matters. Would you know anything about that?"

Darren's face grew pale. "Sensitive matters? I... I'm not sure what you mean."

"Come on, Mr. Blake," Max pressed, his voice dropping a notch. "You're a sharp man. If Emily was looking into things that might be dangerous, you'd have noticed."

Darren shifted uncomfortably, finally sighing. "Look, Emily... she was idealistic, you know? She didn't understand how things really work. The senator tries to keep things clean, but in politics..." He trailed off, visibly uncomfortable. "It's not always black and white."

"What did she know?" Max asked, watching Darren's expression closely.

Darren swallowed, his gaze darting to the floor. "I don't know what she found. But she was talking to people, looking into... things that could threaten her father's reputation. She said the city needed cleansing, like she was some kind of crusader."

"Would her actions have posed a risk to the senator?"

"Possibly," Darren admitted, a hint of bitterness in his voice. "I told her to leave it alone, but she wouldn't listen. She was trying to dig too deep into the city's darker sides, the parts that people in power would prefer to keep hidden."

Max sat back, letting the implications settle. Darren seemed genuinely fearful, almost resentful. His words hinted at deeper motivations, hidden agendas that might have placed Emily directly in harm's way.

"Thank you, Darren. If you think of anything else, don't hesitate to contact me."

Darren nodded quickly, clearly eager to end the conversation. As Max stepped outside, he let the interviews run through his mind. Leah's concern, Jake's bitterness, and Darren's evasiveness had each offered clues but no concrete answers. And yet, a pattern was forming. Emily had indeed been onto something—and whatever it was, it had rattled more than just her inner circle.

But were these simply the people closest to her, or could one of them have known about her plans and taken things a step further?

As twilight settled over Dominion City, Max returned to the spot where Emily Lawson had been abducted. Most of the street had emptied, the sidewalks bathed in the soft glow of street lamps, casting long shadows against the concrete. The café she'd left was now closed, its lights dim, giving the scene an eerie stillness.

Max took a slow, methodical walk around the area. Earlier that morning, police had cordoned off the street, and forensics had done a sweep. Yet, instinct told him there was something overlooked, something no one else would have thought to search for. His years on the force had taught him that the smallest details often held the biggest revelations.

The concrete around the abduction site was marked with subtle scuff marks, evidence of Emily's struggle. Max crouched down, brushing his fingers lightly over a faint trail in the dirt that led to the curb. It was clear that Emily hadn't gone willingly—there were signs of a fight, but what caught his attention was a spot on the wall near the café's entrance, partially hidden by a trash bin. Moving the bin aside, he noticed a faint symbol etched into the wall, almost blending with the grime and graffiti that covered the alley.

The symbol was simple yet precise: three interlocking circles, each containing a different geometric shape—a triangle, a square, and a star. Max frowned, pulling out his phone to snap a picture.

The design was unfamiliar to him, yet something about it struck a chord. He'd seen variations of symbols like this before, usually associated with fringe groups or underground movements. But this symbol seemed unique, intentionally hidden in plain sight as if left by someone who didn't want it widely recognized but hoped certain eyes would understand.

As Max rose, he heard footsteps behind him, and a familiar, unwelcome voice broke the silence.

"Late-night research, Carter? Or are you just wandering around hoping for inspiration?" Adrian Cross stepped into view, smirking, his posture relaxed and his gaze dripping with amusement.

Max clenched his jaw but kept his face neutral. "I'm following leads. You should try it sometime, Cross. You might actually find something useful."

Adrian chuckled, folding his arms as he glanced around the scene. "Following leads? Is that what you call staring at a wall?"

"Some of us look a little closer than others," Max replied, turning back to examine the symbol. Adrian's presence only heightened his irritation, but he refused to let his rival's arrogance cloud his judgment.

Adrian took a step closer, peering at the symbol. "What do you think it is? Gang-related?"

"Doubtful," Max said flatly, pocketing his phone. "Too clean. Too… intentional. Whoever left this knew what they were doing. They wanted it to be found, but not by just anyone."

Adrian shrugged, unimpressed. "I wouldn't waste too much time on it. Probably some wannabe anarchist trying to spook people."

Max turned to face him, his voice steady. "Do you have anything better to contribute, or are you just here to hover?"

Adrian's smile faded slightly, but he kept his composure. "Actually, Carter, I've been busy collecting useful information. Seems Emily Lawson wasn't exactly squeaky clean herself. People around here knew her as an 'activist,' but some of the city's more extreme circles—ones her father isn't too fond of—saw her as an ally."

"Did those 'extreme circles' leave anything specific, or are you still banking on rumors?" Max asked, keeping his tone calm even as his patience wore thin.

"Rumors have led me to more than you'd think," Adrian replied with a sly smile. "Emily was in deep with some anti-establishment types. A little more than her father would want out in the open. I wouldn't be surprised if she staged her own kidnapping, hoping it would fuel her cause."

Max considered the idea, as it wasn't entirely implausible. Emily's connections with activist groups had already raised questions among her acquaintances. But the symbol on the wall and the force used to abduct her suggested otherwise. Whoever took her was not trying to make a public statement. They were precise and prepared—this had been carefully planned, not a reckless act of self-sabotage.

"If she staged her own kidnapping," Max said, looking at Adrian pointedly, "she wouldn't have needed to leave signs of a struggle. And I don't see why she'd leave a symbol behind that looks more like a warning than a calling card."

Adrian scoffed. "Maybe she was leaving breadcrumbs for a political stunt. Or maybe you're just overthinking it, Carter."

Max bit back a retort, reminded himself to stay focused. He turned back to the wall, blocking out Adrian's presence as he examined the symbol once more. His mind whirred with possibilities. He'd dealt with cult-like symbols before, symbols associated with groups that aimed to be invisible while wielding power behind closed doors. His memory traced back to rumors of a secretive organization—a cult of sorts, hiding in the shadows of Dominion City's political and social elite.

He'd never found concrete proof of their existence, but now, standing here, the image before him hinted at their involvement.

"Fine," Adrian said with a dismissive wave. "You stick to your theories, Carter. I'll be following up on actual leads." He turned on his heel, his footsteps echoing as he walked away, leaving Max in the dimly lit alley.

Max felt a prickle of determination and slight unease settle over him as he watched his rival disappear into the darkness. The symbol—its presence gnawed at him, as did Adrian's thinly veiled smugness. It was a reminder of the high stakes at play, and Max was unwilling to let Adrian's short-sighted ambitions derail him.

As he pocketed his phone and turned away from the wall, Max felt a renewed sense of purpose. If Emily Lawson was caught up in something as powerful and insidious as the cult he suspected, then this case was more dangerous than anyone realized. The symbol left behind was no accident; it was a signal—a silent marker of control, warning anyone who might be foolish enough to pry further.

And for Max, that was an invitation he couldn't resist.

Back at the station, Max was deep in thought, running through the clues he had gathered. The strange symbol, the hints of Emily's activist leanings, the nervous responses from those closest to her—it all suggested a much deeper story beneath her disappearance. The pieces felt connected, but he couldn't yet see how they fit together.

Max had just started sifting through old case files involving symbols and fringe groups when the door to his office swung open. Adrian Cross strode in without knocking, a self-satisfied grin on his face as he dropped a stack of papers onto Max's already cluttered desk.

"Thought you might want a look at these," Adrian said, crossing his arms as he leaned against the door frame. "Turns out Emily Lawson was more involved in questionable circles than you think."

Max glanced at the papers, then back at Adrian, barely concealing his irritation. "Is this about her activist work?"

"More than that," Adrian replied, his tone smug. "Seems like she was getting close with a group that's been on the department's watchlist. Radical types—anti-government, anti-corporate. They've been stirring things up on the fringes for a while now."

Max's eyebrows lifted slightly as he leafed through the papers. Reports on recent protests, graffiti markings around the city, small skirmishes with law enforcement—Emily's name was nowhere in the files, but her presence in those circles wasn't hard to imagine. He took a closer look, noting that some of the group's rhetoric touched on corruption within the city's political system, echoing the things he'd heard from Leah and Darren.

"And you think this means she staged her own kidnapping?" Max asked, trying to keep his voice neutral as he looked up at Adrian.

Adrian shrugged. "It's a theory. She's young, idealistic. Maybe she got in over her head, wanted to make a splash and thought this would be her way out. We've seen it before—people with too much ambition and not enough sense."

Max resisted the urge to roll his eyes. Adrian always preferred the simplest solution, especially when it fit neatly into a narrative that he could sell to his superiors. But Max couldn't shake the feeling that this wasn't the case with Emily. Her disappearance had been too clean, too precise. Whoever had taken her hadn't left much behind.

"Interesting theory," Max said finally, his voice carefully even. "But it doesn't explain the symbol at the crime scene."

Adrian's smirk faded, his eyes narrowing. "Symbol? What symbol?"

Max gave a slight, satisfied smile. "Guess you missed that part. There was a mark near the café where she was taken. Looked like it was carved intentionally, almost like a message."

Adrian's eyes flashed with irritation. "You think it's connected to her activist friends?"

"It doesn't fit their usual style," Max said, watching Adrian closely. "It's more... specific. Less of a public statement, more of a warning."

Adrian's jaw tightened, and for a moment, the easy confidence that he wore like armor seemed to slip. "Or maybe you're seeing what you want to see, Carter. I think you're making this more complicated than it is. We have a young woman with a hero complex, ties to radical circles, and the desire to make a point. This could just as easily be a self-made spectacle gone wrong."

Max met Adrian's gaze, refusing to back down. "Maybe. Or maybe you're just ignoring the facts that don't fit into your version of events."

The tension between them thickened, each man holding his ground. Max could see the frustration simmering beneath Adrian's mask of confidence, and it gave him a small, fleeting sense of satisfaction. But he knew that the stakes were too high to let their rivalry cloud his judgment. He needed to stay focused, to dig deeper and uncover the truth—no matter where it led.

Adrian finally broke the silence, scoffing as he pushed himself off the door frame. "Suit yourself, Carter. Just don't get lost chasing ghosts. We both know the higher-ups want this wrapped up quickly, and I won't hesitate to do what it takes to make that happen."

With that, he turned on his heel and walked out, leaving Max alone with the files. As the door clicked shut, Max let out a slow breath, allowing himself a moment to process the encounter. Adrian was as insistent as ever on taking the fastest route to a solution, but Max couldn't ignore the feeling gnawing at him—the sense that there was something lurking beneath the surface, a shadowy force that was carefully orchestrating events from behind the scenes.

Emily Lawson wasn't just a young woman with idealistic ambitions. Whatever she'd uncovered, whatever connections she had made, they were dangerous enough to provoke a swift, calculated response. The symbol near the café haunted him, each interlocking shape seeming to mock his search for answers. He was on the edge of something bigger, something that had been brewing beneath Dominion City's surface for far too long.

Glancing back down at the files Adrian had left, Max steeled himself. This wasn't just about solving a case. It was about peeling back the layers of the city's darkest secrets, exposing the hidden forces pulling the strings.

If Adrian wanted a quick and tidy resolution, he could chase his own theories. But Max was prepared to go wherever the evidence took him—no matter how deep or dangerous the path became.

Back at his apartment later that night, Max paced around his small living room, his mind racing. Adrian's theory about Emily staging her own kidnapping kept echoing in his mind, gnawing at him despite his better judgment. While the idea seemed thin, he couldn't ignore the mounting circumstantial evidence linking Emily to activist circles that often leaned into public stunts and displays.

Max spread a collection of files across his coffee table, scrutinizing each report that Adrian had dropped off. The documents detailed the activities of a few activist groups operating within Dominion City—mostly youth-driven movements that had been protesting against corruption, inequality, and the influence of big money on politics. Their rhetoric was bold, but Max had never seen any indication they'd take it this far. Still, the thought lingered: Could Emily have orchestrated her own abduction to make a political statement?

Max sat down, flipping through each report carefully, paying attention to the dates of recent protests and public statements by some of Dominion City's more vocal agitators. One name kept popping up—a group called The Dominion Watch. Their manifesto was scattered across social media, targeting the city's politicians and corporate elites with accusations of bribery, extortion, and backdoor deals. Emily's father, Senator Lawson, was mentioned frequently in their posts, often as a central symbol of the city's corruption.

He took a deep breath and reviewed some police reports from previous encounters with the Dominion Watch at protests. They were small but determined, a group fueled by indignation, and their tactics had recently shifted to more aggressive actions: vandalism, threats, and confrontations with law enforcement. But everything he read suggested that they were only a nuisance—not a serious threat.

Yet one report caught his attention: An anonymous tip had been submitted a week before Emily's abduction, claiming that "a major event" was being planned, something that would "expose Dominion City's true face to the world." The language was vague, but the implication was unmistakable. If this group was involved in Emily's disappearance, it could indeed be a high-stakes performance designed to embarrass the city's power brokers, especially her father.

Max leaned back, running a hand through his hair as he considered the possibility. Maybe Adrian was right, in part. Maybe Emily had joined the Dominion Watch or was working with a similar group, and perhaps she thought a staged kidnapping could give them the platform they wanted. But something didn't sit right.

If this were a stunt, why had there been no demand, no message to the public, no manifesto claiming responsibility? The entire city was already in a panic, with the media covering every angle of her disappearance. A staged event would typically culminate in a reveal, a dramatic proclamation of purpose, but so far—nothing.

Lost in thought, Max was startled by the sudden ring of his phone. He picked it up, recognizing the number as that of Leah Brighton, Emily's close friend whom he had interviewed earlier.

"Leah," he answered, his voice calm but curious.

"Detective Carter," Leah's voice was barely a whisper, thick with fear. "I'm sorry to call so late... but I just found something, and... I think you should know about it."

"What is it?" he asked, leaning forward.

"Emily had a journal," Leah said, her words tumbling out in a rush. "She never let anyone see it, but tonight... I remembered where she hid it. I went through it, and there's something strange in it."

Max's pulse quickened. "Go on."

"There are pages... names, dates, places she went to. She was following people, Detective. She was... scared. She didn't write much, but she mentioned someone called *The Architect*." Leah's voice quivered, and Max could hear the anxiety in her tone. "It's... it's like she was onto something big. Something dangerous."

"The Architect?" Max repeated, his mind racing as he tried to connect this new information with the symbol at the crime scene. "Did she write anything else about him?"

"Just... just that he was dangerous. That he knew things about her father, and about Dominion City's secrets." Leah hesitated, and Max could almost feel her shudder over the line. "Detective, I don't think this was a stunt. Emily was scared of him."

Max's grip tightened on the phone. Leah's words confirmed his suspicions—Emily hadn't staged her disappearance. She had been in way over her head, and it seemed the threat was far more real than anyone had guessed.

"Where are you now, Leah?" Max asked, standing up and grabbing his coat.

"I'm at home," she whispered. "I didn't know who else to call..."

"Stay there. Don't talk to anyone else about this, understand? I'll be there shortly," Max said firmly. Leah agreed, and he hung up, pocketing his phone as he left his apartment.

The night air was thick as Max drove to Leah's apartment, the symbol from the crime scene replaying in his mind along with the name *The Architect*. Whoever this person was, he seemed to be at the center of Emily's fears, someone she believed had the power to harm her and, potentially, anyone close to her.

As he pulled up to Leah's building, he couldn't shake the ominous feeling that had settled over him. There was something here that went beyond simple political activism, a dark thread woven into the city's core.

Leah was waiting at her door when he arrived, clutching a worn leather-bound journal tightly against her chest. Her face was pale, her eyes wide with fear.

"Detective," she whispered, handing him the journal. "I... I didn't know she was this involved."

Max took the journal, feeling the weight of the responsibility, it carried. He opened it carefully, flipping through the pages filled with Emily's neat handwriting, annotated with dates and cryptic notations about meetings and surveillance. Her words hinted at shadows in places he hadn't known to look before—mentions of figures in dark coats, meetings held in hidden basements, cryptic whispers of Dominion City's "unseen hands."

Then he found it, scrawled hastily across a page toward the end of the journal: *The Architect. If he finds out I know... I don't know what he'll do. But he's always watching. He knows everything.*

Max glanced up at Leah, who was watching him with anxious eyes. "Did Emily ever mention this to you before?"

Leah shook her head, her hands trembling slightly. "No... but she always seemed on edge. She would say things about her father's world being a 'house of cards,' about people she didn't trust. I thought she was just frustrated with politics; you know?"

Max nodded, feeling a chill settle in his bones. Whatever Emily had uncovered, it wasn't just a political protest gone wrong. She had uncovered something dangerous—something powerful enough to make her feel hunted.

And somewhere out there, *The Architect* was watching.

Chapter 2: Shadows in Power

Senator Robert Lawson's office sat like a fortress in Dominion City's government district, housed in a towering building with security that seemed a little too intense for a senator's workspace. As Max Carter entered the reception area, he was met with the polished gleam of marble floors, leather seating, and an air of formality that felt impenetrable.

A receptionist led Max down a long corridor to a wide mahogany door. She knocked twice before opening it, gesturing for him to enter. Max stepped inside, his gaze sweeping over the elegant space—shelves filled with carefully chosen books, framed certificates, and photos from various political events that decorated the walls. Senator Lawson sat behind a large desk, his face drawn and his posture tense, yet he managed a professional smile as Max approached.

"Detective Carter," Lawson greeted him, rising from his chair with an outstretched hand. "Thank you for coming. Anything I can do to help bring my daughter home, you'll have it."

Max shook his hand, noting the firm grip and the brief eye contact before Lawson glanced away. He took a seat across from the senator, leaning forward slightly as he began his questions.

"Senator Lawson," Max began, keeping his voice steady, "I understand that this is a difficult time, but I need to ask some questions about Emily's recent activities. Anything unusual she was involved in? People she may have mentioned?"

Lawson shifted uncomfortably, glancing at his hands before looking up. "Emily is... was... very independent. She didn't always share what she was up to, especially recently. I know she was passionate, determined to bring attention to causes she believed in, but that's always been her nature."

Max kept his gaze steady. "Were there any specific causes she was focused on? Anything that might have stirred conflict?"

The senator paused, choosing his words carefully. "She's always been driven to improve this city, and she saw injustice everywhere. She'd sometimes get involved in activist circles, rallies—idealistic stuff. But she never took it too far. At least, I didn't think so."

Max didn't break eye contact. "Senator, I have reason to believe Emily was involved with people who weren't just activists. There's evidence suggesting she was researching groups with a reputation for secrecy. Does that sound familiar?"

Lawson's mouth tightened. He leaned back in his chair, his eyes narrowing slightly as he processed Max's words. "Detective, Emily's interests in social justice sometimes… attracted people with radical ideas. I can't say I agreed with everything she got involved in, but she was a young woman finding her own way."

Max watched him, noting the senator's carefully measured responses. Lawson was talking, but he was saying as little as possible, choosing each word with precision. There was an undertone of defensiveness in his voice, a subtle tension that suggested he was holding something back.

Max pressed on. "Did she mention anyone specific? She was connected to a journalist, Sarah Blane, who indicated Emily had been looking into a group called 'The Sovereigns.' Does that ring any bells?"

At the mention of The Sovereigns, Lawson's face grew pale. He shifted in his chair, casting a quick glance toward his assistant, Darren, who stood quietly in the corner of the room, watching the exchange with a stoic expression. The brief exchange of looks between them didn't escape Max's notice.

"I... I don't know anything about that," Lawson replied, his tone slightly unsteady. "I've heard rumors of groups operating in Dominion City, but nothing substantiated. Certainly not anything my daughter would involve herself with."

Max leaned forward, letting the silence stretch, hoping the discomfort would coax the senator into revealing more. But Lawson quickly gathered himself, sitting up straighter, his face returning to its controlled, polished look. "Emily was no radical, Detective. She was young and passionate, yes, but not reckless."

Max made a note of the senator's reaction and changed tactics. "Has anyone been in contact with you since she disappeared? Any messages, threats, or ransom demands?"

"No." Lawson's response was immediate, but the tension in his shoulders belied his calm tone. "Nothing. It's as if she vanished into thin air."

Max's gaze drifted over to Darren, who had been silent the entire time. "And you, Mr. Blake? Did Emily ever mention anything unusual to you? Any concerns about people she might have been dealing with?"

Darren glanced at Lawson before answering, a nervous flicker in his eyes. "Emily was... outspoken. She wasn't afraid to challenge people. Sometimes she'd express... frustrations with the city's leadership. She believed that real change needed to happen, and I think she felt strongly about making her voice heard."

Lawson interrupted, his tone firm. "Emily is passionate, Detective. She wanted to see the world become a better place, that's all. If she seemed outspoken, it was only because she cared."

But Max could tell from the way Lawson had said it—as if trying to convince himself—that there was more to the story. He nodded, keeping his voice neutral. "I appreciate your cooperation, Senator. We'll do everything in our power to find her."

Lawson's jaw tightened, his eyes dropping to the desk before he spoke. "I know this city, Detective. I know the people in it. Whoever took Emily... they're playing a dangerous game. I don't know what they want from her, but I promise you, I will not let them get away with it."

Max met his gaze, feeling the weight of Lawson's words. He had no doubt the senator would throw his entire influence into recovering his daughter, but there was something unsettling in his demeanor. Max sensed that Lawson was concealing something—a fear or knowledge that he wasn't willing to share. Whether it was to protect Emily, his career, or himself, Max couldn't be sure.

As he stood to leave, Lawson spoke once more. "Detective Carter," he said, his voice lower, almost cautious, "if you find out who's behind this... you'll let me know, won't you?"

Max paused, looking back at Lawson. "You'll know as soon as we have any leads, Senator. You have my word."

He nodded, but something dark flickered in his eyes before he turned back to his assistant, dismissing Max with a curt nod.

As Max stepped out of the office, his thoughts churned with questions. Lawson's polished exterior masked layers of complexity, and the silent exchange between him and Darren hadn't gone unnoticed. The senator was afraid of something or someone—and if Max's suspicions were right, it wasn't just Emily's safety at risk. Whatever connections Emily had uncovered, whatever truths she'd been chasing, they ran deeper than her father was willing to admit.

Max walked down the long corridor, his footsteps echoing as he headed toward the exit. Outside the government building, the city stretched out before him, its gleaming towers and dark alleys concealing secrets just waiting to be unearthed.

The exclusive Dominion Club was an elite retreat where the city's influential figures met behind closed doors, a sanctuary for politicians, business moguls, and social heavyweights. Located on the top floor of a historic building, it boasted dark wood-paneled walls, velvet seating, and a view of the city that was both stunning and intimidating. Tonight, the club was quiet, its usual clientele absent, making it an ideal place for a private conversation.

Detective Adrian Cross walked through the lobby with a confident stride, his sharp suit pressed to perfection and his gaze intense. The manager, a discreet man who recognized Adrian's face, nodded and led him down a hall, opening the door to a secluded parlor room where Councilman Paul Haynes was waiting. Haynes, a slim, nervous-looking man with slicked-back gray hair and a perpetual frown, glanced up, irritation flickering across his face as Adrian entered.

"Councilman Haynes," Adrian greeted him with a charming yet calculated smile. "I appreciate you taking the time. I understand this isn't easy, but we both want to find Emily, don't we?"

Haynes shifted uncomfortably in his chair, folding his hands. "Detective Cross," he said, his tone cold, "I'm not sure why you wanted to meet here. Surely, we could have discussed this somewhere more... appropriate."

Adrian ignored the complaint, taking a seat across from him, his posture relaxed but his eyes sharp. "I thought a place like this might be more convenient for you, Councilman. After all, this is where the city's real business happens, isn't it?"

Haynes bristled, his jaw tightening. "I'm a public servant, Detective. I don't indulge in these conspiracy theories. If you're here to accuse me of something, I suggest you get to the point."

Adrian held up his hands, his voice smooth. "I'm not here to accuse anyone, Councilman. But I do need to ask you some questions about Emily Lawson. We both know she wasn't just a senator's daughter—she had connections, and she wasn't afraid to use them."

Haynes's eyes darted to the door, as if making sure it was closed. His voice dropped, a note of irritation creeping in. "Emily was... ambitious, I'll give her that. Her idealism was admirable, but often misguided. She couldn't understand that change doesn't come from throwing stones. She was more like her mother that way."

Adrian's eyes sharpened, catching the councilman's brief look of sadness, but he pressed on. "Misguided, perhaps, but effective. She was good at making people talk, wasn't she? Rumor has it she attended a few... exclusive gatherings recently. Meetings involving people of your stature, Councilman."

Haynes's lips thinned; his face clouded with irritation. "Emily was a young woman seeking thrills. I can't control who she associates with, and neither can her father. As for those gatherings," he added dismissively, "they were private social events. Harmless."

Adrian leaned forward; his gaze unyielding. "Harmless, maybe, but it's interesting. Just a few days after these events, she disappears. Do you really think that's a coincidence?"

Haynes looked away, fidgeting with the cufflinks on his shirt. Adrian could sense the councilman's discomfort growing, and he pressed harder, determined to get answers.

"Come on, Councilman. These gatherings—she wasn't just there for cocktails, was she?" Adrian's voice dropped, his tone hardening. "Did she confront anyone? Threaten to expose something?"

Haynes shifted uncomfortably, finally breaking his silence. "Fine. I'll tell you this much," he muttered. "Emily had a way of asking the wrong questions. I saw her... speaking to certain people. People she shouldn't have been associating with."

"Who?" Adrian pressed, his pulse quickening.

Haynes hesitated, his gaze darting to the window. "There's a group in this city... people who don't operate by ordinary rules. They call themselves... well, I've heard whispers. They call themselves 'The Sovereigns.' But they're no mere club. They're powerful, and they don't appreciate nosy outsiders. Emily... she was asking too many questions."

Adrian felt a jolt of excitement. The Sovereigns—a name he'd heard mentioned in only the darkest circles, always shrouded in rumor and conspiracy. He fought to keep his expression neutral, though his mind raced with the implications.

"Are you saying this group is involved in her disappearance?" he asked, keeping his tone steady, careful not to reveal his eagerness.

"I don't know anything concrete," Haynes said quickly, his voice dropping to a whisper. "But I know enough to stay away. If Emily crossed them, well... she'd be in serious danger. This is a group that's existed in the city's shadows for decades. They have influence in places people like you wouldn't imagine."

Adrian's eyes narrowed. "And you just let her walk into that? Let her attend those parties, knowing who might be there?"

Haynes bristled, sitting up straight. "I wasn't her keeper, Detective. Emily was smart and strong-willed. She thought she could handle herself." His gaze shifted, the irritation in his eyes replaced with something closer to guilt. "I may have tried to warn her once... but she didn't listen."

Adrian watched Haynes carefully, reading the flickers of guilt and fear in the councilman's face. He leaned in, his voice low and intense. "Who leads this group? Who in those circles would want Emily gone?"

Haynes hesitated, his mouth opening as if to answer, but he quickly shook his head. "I can't say any more. I don't know much else, and frankly, I don't want to."

"Look, Councilman," Adrian said, his tone growing colder, "if you know something that could lead us to Emily, then withholding it isn't just reckless—it's criminal."

Haynes's expression hardened, his eyes meeting Adrian's with defiance. "I've told you all I can, Detective. Anything further, and I'd be risking my career. Or worse."

He rose from his seat, signaling the end of their conversation, but Adrian remained seated, his gaze fixed on the councilman. "You know, this group of yours may think they're untouchable, but they've made a mistake. We'll find Emily, and when we do, every one of you will be brought to justice."

Haynes's face remained impassive, but Adrian caught a glimmer of unease in his eyes. Without another word, the councilman turned and left the room, leaving Adrian alone in the quiet parlor. The silence felt charged, filled with the weight of what he had just uncovered.

Adrian leaned back, the name "The Sovereigns" echoing in his mind. He'd never had the chance to pursue them before, but this case might finally give him the opportunity he'd been waiting for. He'd need to tread carefully, but with a group as powerful as The Sovereigns, a mistake could be fatal. He didn't have many allies in

Dominion City, but he didn't need allies—just the drive to see his ambitions through.

As Adrian stood to leave, he allowed himself a small smile. Whatever secrets lay hidden among the city's elite; he would bring them to light. And if The Sovereigns wanted to keep those secrets buried, they'd have to go through him.

Back at his cluttered office, Detective Max Carter sat reviewing the notes he'd taken during his conversation with Senator Lawson. Every answer the senator had given was guarded, every expression carefully controlled, yet Max sensed that underneath the polished exterior, Lawson was hiding something that could be vital to the investigation.

As he scanned the pages, he was interrupted by a knock at the door. He looked up, surprised to see Sarah Blane standing there, clutching a worn leather satchel to her chest. The young journalist looked anxious. Dark circles under her eyes suggested sleepless nights, and her posture was tense, as if she expected someone to jump out at her.

"Detective Carter," she whispered, glancing over her shoulder before stepping inside and closing the door quickly. "Thank you for seeing me."

Max stood and gestured for her to sit, studying her closely. "Sarah, what's going on? You look like you haven't slept in days."

"I haven't," she admitted, dropping the satchel onto his desk with a trembling hand. "Ever since Emily disappeared, I've felt like someone's watching me. I can't explain it, but I feel like... like I'm in danger too."

Max's eyes sharpened as he leaned forward. "Danger from whom?"

"The Sovereigns," she whispered, her face pale. "Emily... she left these for me. She said if anything happened to her, I should bring them to you."

Max felt a chill creep up his spine. He opened the satchel carefully, revealing a set of neatly folded notes and a small leather-bound notebook, worn from use. The pages were filled with Emily's handwriting—tight, controlled, and methodical. Each page contained observations, meeting details, and initials next to dates and locations that immediately caught his eye.

"Emily was investigating The Sovereigns?" Max asked, flipping through the notes with intense focus.

Sarah nodded, biting her lip. "Yes. She'd been trying to get close to them for months. I thought it was just... her usual sense of idealism. But it got serious. She kept telling me that there was something sinister about them, something connected to her father's political career. She was gathering evidence that could bring them down."

Max's pulse quickened as he skimmed the pages. He came across cryptic phrases Emily had written: *"Secrets in the shadows," "The unseen hand," "Loyalty above all else."* Names were scribbled here and there—some partially obscured by frantic pen marks, as if Emily had worried about leaving them visible even in her own notes.

Then, a familiar title jumped out at him: *The Architect*. Next to it, Emily had drawn a small symbol that matched the one he'd found at the crime scene—the three interlocking circles, each containing a shape: a triangle, a square, and a star.

Max looked up, locking eyes with Sarah. "Did she ever mention this person—the Architect?"

"Only a little," Sarah whispered, shivering despite the warmth of the office. "She said he was the one who held it all together. That he was the heart of The Sovereigns, the person everyone looked up to. She thought he knew about her investigation and that he'd do anything to stop her."

Max's fingers tightened around the notebook. If Emily had uncovered the true identity of this Architect, then her disappearance was no random act—it was a targeted move, a way to keep her silent before she could expose what she knew.

"She was onto something big, wasn't she?" Max muttered, half to himself.

Sarah nodded. "Yes, and she was terrified. She told me she felt like she was being watched, like someone was following her. But she wouldn't stop. She said she had to know the truth, even if it was dangerous."

Max thumbed through another page and found a list of names with corresponding initials. A few he recognized, including Councilman Haynes, but several others were unfamiliar. "These names," he murmured, more to himself. "They must be connected to The Sovereigns. Did she ever tell you anything specific about them? Their meetings, their rituals?"

"She mentioned a few things." Sarah's voice dropped to a near whisper. "She said they had rituals that bound them to each other. She'd heard they called it a 'renewal of loyalty' or something like that. She thought it was more than just a ceremony—that it was a way to keep their secrets buried, to make sure no one would ever betray them."

Max's mind raced as he pieced together the information. If The Sovereigns used these rituals to cement loyalty among their members, then Emily's investigation threatened more than just one individual—it threatened a network that could unravel Dominion City's political elite.

Sarah's hand shook as she reached into her satchel again, pulling out a small, folded piece of paper. "There's one more thing. Emily left this for me the night before she disappeared. She said I should memorize it and then destroy it, but... I kept it."

Max took the paper and opened it carefully. Scrawled in Emily's handwriting was a list of locations: an abandoned warehouse, a private estate in the hills, and the Dominion Club. Next to each was a date, including one marked for the coming Friday—a day from now.

"These are meeting places?" Max asked, his voice tight with urgency.

Sarah nodded. "She thought these were sites where The Sovereigns gathered. She was going to follow them, gather more proof."

Max felt a chill settle over him as he looked at the final location on the list: the Dominion Club, the same place Adrian had questioned Councilman Haynes earlier. If Emily's suspicions were correct, then the Sovereigns' leadership, including this mysterious Architect, could be hiding in plain sight, right in the heart of Dominion City.

"You have to be careful, Detective," Sarah whispered, her voice trembling. "If they find out you know this much, they'll come after you, too. They don't care who they hurt to keep their secrets safe."

Max closed the notebook, a dark resolve settling over him. "If Emily's still out there, I'll find her. And I won't stop until I know what these people are hiding."

He stood, looking down at Sarah. "Thank you for trusting me with this," he said, his tone softening slightly. "You've done the right thing."

She gave him a faint, sad smile, her hands wringing nervously. "I just want to see her safe, Detective. She's... she's my best friend. I don't know what I'll do if—" Her voice cracked, and she swallowed, blinking back tears.

Max placed a reassuring hand on her shoulder. "I'll do everything I can. Now, go home, and stay alert. If you notice anything unusual, call me immediately. Don't take any chances."

Sarah nodded, her gaze fixed on the floor as she quickly exited, leaving Max alone with the evidence she'd brought. As he examined Emily's notes again, he felt the weight of the city's secrets pressing down on him. The Sovereigns weren't just some myths whispered about in conspiracy circles—they were real, and they wielded power far beyond his reach.

But Max couldn't turn back now. Emily had left a trail, and he intended to follow it, no matter how dangerous the path.

With a grim sense of determination, he tucked the notes into a folder, mentally preparing himself for what lay ahead. If The Sovereigns thought they could keep their secrets buried, they were about to learn just how far he was willing to go to unearth the truth.

Max made his way to the towering Dominion Corporate Plaza, an office high-rise that was home to some of the city's most powerful business figures. Inside one of its luxurious offices was Douglas Reyland, a wealthy businessman and longtime financial backer of Senator Lawson. Reyland's name had come up repeatedly in Emily's notes as well as from Adrian's aggressive questioning of Lawson's inner circle. But it wasn't until Max received a tip that

Reyland had been seen deleting messages and avoiding contact with the police that he decided to investigate further.

Reyland's office was on the 38th floor, a pristine space with floor-to-ceiling windows that looked out over Dominion City. Max waited in the plush lobby as Reyland's assistant, a young woman with a nervous smile, informed him that Reyland would be available shortly. As she left to announce his arrival, Max caught sight of Adrian Cross stepping out of the elevator, a smug look on his face.

"Well, well, Carter," Adrian greeted with a casual grin. "Didn't expect to see you here. Thought I'd beat you to the punch."

Max suppressed a sigh, turning to face his rival with a forced smile. "I'm just here to follow up on a lead. It's not a competition, Cross."

Adrian chuckled, straightening his suit jacket. "Oh, but isn't it? Reyland's got his hands in just about every dirty deal in Dominion. We both know he's hiding something. Question is, will you find it before I do?"

Max ignored the taunt and turned his focus back to the case at hand. Before he could respond, the assistant reappeared, gesturing for both detectives to enter Reyland's office.

Inside, Douglas Reyland sat behind a massive desk, his dark hair graying at the temples and his expression one of carefully maintained composure. He gave both men a curt nod as they entered, but his gaze remained cool, revealing nothing. Max noted the lines of tension around Reyland's mouth and the way his fingers drummed on his desk—a small, involuntary habit that hinted at his nervousness.

"Detectives," Reyland began, his voice steady but forced. "What brings you here today?"

Max didn't waste time on pleasantries. "We have a few questions regarding your recent communication with Senator Lawson and, potentially, his daughter Emily."

Reyland's eyes narrowed, his expression hardening. "Emily? What does she have to do with my business?"

Max exchanged a brief glance with Adrian, who seemed content to let him take the lead for now. "Sources indicate that you were one of the last people in contact with her before she disappeared," Max continued, keeping his tone calm but probing. "Witnesses say you've been deleting texts and avoiding questions about her disappearance. Care to explain?"

Reyland's jaw tightened, and his hands stopped drumming. He leaned back, adopting a defensive posture. "This is absurd," he replied, his voice laced with irritation. "Emily was like family to me. I would never harm her. If I deleted any messages, it was because I handle sensitive business matters, none of which are related to her disappearance."

Adrian, spoke his tone sharper. "We know you attended the same exclusive gatherings Emily was at, Reyland. Those private events—where only the elite of Dominion City are invited. Care to tell us what goes on at those events?"

Reyland's face grew even paler. "Those are social gatherings," he said quickly, his gaze darting between the two detectives. "There's nothing sinister about them. Just business talk, harmless mingling."

Max raised an eyebrow, not buying the response. "Mingling? Interesting choice of words. We have sources suggesting that these gatherings are tied to The Sovereigns—an organization that doesn't exactly have a spotless reputation."

At the mention of The Sovereigns, a flash of fear crossed Reyland's face, and he quickly looked away. The reaction was brief, but telling. Max's suspicions deepened; Reyland was clearly more entangled with The Sovereigns than he was willing to admit.

"Look," Reyland said, his voice quieter now, almost pleading. "I'm not part of any cult, Detective. Yes, I've attended certain gatherings, but they're nothing more than networking events. People talk, they exchange ideas. That's all."

Adrian leaned forward, pressing harder. "Then why were you deleting messages? If there's nothing to hide, why the secrecy?"

Reyland's assistant entered the room then, carrying a small stack of papers, but Max's attention was immediately drawn to her hand. In her nervousness, she fumbled, and a USB drive slipped from the papers, clattering onto the desk. Reyland shot her a warning look as she quickly retrieved it, her hands shaking slightly.

Max caught Adrian's gaze, and they both exchanged a look of silent understanding.

"I think we'll need to take that USB drive with us," Max said, his tone polite but firm.

Reyland's face went rigid. "Those files are confidential. They have nothing to do with this investigation."

Adrian stepped in, his tone cold and unyielding. "We'll be the judges of that, Mr. Reyland. Hand it over."

Reyland's face twisted in frustration, but he nodded to his assistant, who reluctantly handed the USB drive to Max. She gave Reyland an apologetic glance before hurrying out of the room, clearly eager to escape the tension.

Max pocketed the drive, giving Reyland a steady look. "If there's anything on here that indicates illegal activity or connections to Emily's disappearance, we'll know about it. Deleting texts and withholding information only make you look more suspicious."

Reyland clenched his jaw, his eyes narrowing. "You're making a mistake, Detective. I've done nothing wrong."

Adrian's smile was anything but friendly. "We'll see about that."

They left the office, and as soon as the door closed behind them, Adrian turned to Max, his smugness back in full force. "Think we'll find anything useful on that drive?"

Max shrugged, though he could feel his own curiosity simmering. "It's hard to say. Reyland's good at covering his tracks. But something doesn't add up."

Adrian smirked. "Maybe he's just hiding some run-of-the-mill financial crimes. People like him always have skeletons in the closet."

"Maybe," Max replied, though he wasn't convinced. The reaction Reyland had shown when they mentioned The Sovereigns wasn't the response of a man simply hiding financial dealings. There was a deeper fear there, something Max was certain was connected to Emily and The Sovereigns.

Later, back at the station, Max plugged the USB drive into his computer. The drive was encrypted, requiring the tech team to crack the files. While he waited, he sifted through Reyland's deleted texts, recently retrieved by the department's cyber unit.

Most of the messages seemed innocuous—meetings, deals, social events. But one message thread stood out, exchanged between Reyland and an unknown contact only days before Emily's disappearance.

The messages were brief but chilling:

- Unknown Contact: "She knows too much. If she keeps digging, it could compromise us all."
- Reyland: "It's under control. She won't be a problem."

Max felt a cold anger surge through him. This exchange, while cryptic, suggested that Reyland knew more about Emily's investigation than he'd admitted. He'd been actively involved in keeping her silent. Whether he had planned her disappearance or had simply been aware of the danger she faced, he was complicit.

Adrian glanced over Max's shoulder, reading the exchange, and whistled softly. "Looks like you were right. Reyland's hands are dirty. If he didn't take Emily himself, he knows exactly who did."

Max gritted his teeth. "This isn't just about Reyland. There's a network here, a whole organization working together to protect their secrets. Emily was onto something big, and Reyland knows who's behind it."

As he closed the file, he thought of Sarah's warning about The Sovereigns and the dark power they wielded over Dominion City. The closer he got to the truth, the more dangerous this case became. But Max was past the point of no return.

No matter how powerful these people were, no matter how deep their roots in the city ran, he was determined to bring them to justice—and to find Emily, whatever it took.

The police evidence room was dimly lit, the air heavy with the scent of stale coffee and paper. Detective Max Carter sat alone at a desk cluttered with files and photos, his brow furrowed in concentration as he sifted through a fresh set of surveillance images. The photos, provided by an informant whose name had been withheld for security, showed a recent gathering of Dominion City's elite—a private event held only two weeks before Emily's disappearance.

The room was silent except for the soft shuffle of paper as Max scanned each photograph, hoping for a clue. His eyes paused on an image showing a grand ballroom filled with formally dressed men and women, all smiles, as they mingled around tables adorned with elaborate floral centerpieces. Crystal chandeliers sparkled overhead, casting a warm glow over the faces in the crowd. He recognized several prominent figures: Councilman Haynes, Douglas Reyland, and others he'd seen at press conferences and city functions. They were men and women with power, influence, and secrets that rarely saw the light of day.

Max continued flipping through the photos until one in particular caught his eye. He leaned forward, squinting as he focused on the lower left corner of the image. There, standing slightly apart from the crowd, was Emily Lawson, dressed in an elegant black gown, her face lit with a smile that didn't reach her eyes. She appeared to be in conversation with a tall, shadowy figure whose face was partially obscured by a column in the background. He wore an unusual pendant that hung from a thick chain around his neck: three interlocking circles, each containing a different shape—a triangle, a square, and a star.

Max's heartbeat quickened. It was the same symbol he'd found etched into the wall near the crime scene, the same strange emblem Sarah had shown him in Emily's notes. The presence of this man, so close to Emily in these final weeks, could not be a coincidence. He studied the pendant, the interlocking shapes almost hypnotic in their complexity, and felt a surge of determination. Whoever this man was, he was almost certainly connected to The Sovereigns—and to Emily's disappearance.

He flipped to the next few photos, his suspicion growing with each one. The images painted a curious scene: Emily appeared again in various parts of the room, mingling with several people, each interaction seeming oddly strained. Her eyes looked wary, her body language subtly defensive, as if she were trying to gather information without giving herself away. He noticed that in each image, her gaze often flickered toward the pendant-wearing man, who seemed to stay at the edges of the crowd, observing, his face hidden in shadow.

Max's suspicions deepened as he noticed other guests clustered around the pendant-wearing figure, their heads bowed as they spoke in hushed tones, often glancing over their shoulders, as though they were constantly on guard. It was clear these people weren't just there for idle conversation. Some of them exchanged briefcases, others handed over small envelopes, and more than one person walked off to isolated corners, disappearing from view altogether.

There was something sinister in the air that night, something Emily must have sensed.

Max scrutinized the pendant-wearing man further, noting the sharpness of his suit and the way his presence seemed to command respect, even if he lingered on the fringes. There was no obvious label for the man in the photos, no name, no identification—just a towering figure with a symbol that represented The Sovereigns' hidden hand.

He flipped through a few more photos, trying to pinpoint familiar faces, anything that could shed light on what Emily had seen that night. Councilman Haynes appeared in several frames, and each time, his gaze was firmly fixed on the pendant-wearing man, as if seeking silent approval. Douglas Reyland was there too, talking to an unknown woman while occasionally glancing toward Emily and the man. Max had seen enough evidence to suspect Reyland's involvement with The Sovereigns, but this event revealed that he was more deeply connected than Max had realized.

Emily had been walking on dangerous ground.

He stared at the pendant again, his mind racing as he pieced together everything he knew about The Sovereigns. This was no ordinary group, and the people gathered here were no ordinary allies. The Sovereigns were an invisible empire, a network bound not just by wealth but by fear and control, with rituals and loyalty tests designed to root out the weak and bind members with secrets that no one could afford to reveal.

Max felt a chill. If Emily had uncovered even a fraction of their influence, she would have been seen as a threat. She'd been out of her depth, unwelcome in a world where questioning anything could have fatal consequences.

Then, as he reached the last photo, Max's gaze locked onto an unsettling detail. In this image, taken from a different angle, he could clearly see the pendant-wearing man watching Emily from a distance. His face was still partially obscured, but his stance—rigid, vigilant—suggested he'd known she was there, known she was watching. He'd likely been keeping an eye on her, aware of her every move.

Max's mind raced with possibilities. Emily must have suspected that someone was following her, that her every step was being tracked. She'd been inching too close to the truth, and The Sovereigns, led by this pendant-wearing man, had been closing in on her, waiting for the right moment to make her disappear.

He carefully placed the photos back in their folder, his resolve hardening. He needed to identify this man. The symbol on his pendant would lead him to the heart of this conspiracy, to the man who called himself *The Architect*, and, with any luck, to Emily.

Max pocketed the folder, feeling the weight of the photos like a silent warning. Every step deeper into this case brought him closer to the edge, to a world where The Sovereigns' power held the city in its grip. And now he was part of it, walking the same path that Emily had walked, risking the same dangers that had led to her disappearance.

But Max didn't hesitate. He had come too far, and he wasn't about to back down. Whoever this man was, he had answers. And Max was prepared to pursue him, no matter how close to danger it brought him.

As he left the evidence room, a feeling settled over him—a sense that eyes were already on him, that the invisible hand of The Sovereigns was ready to tighten around him, if he got too close.

Chapter 3: A Network of Lies

The city's lights were just beginning to flicker on as Detective Max Carter returned to Senator Lawson's office for a follow-up. A trusted member of Lawson's staff, Carla Mitchell, had reached out to Max privately, claiming to have information that might "change the direction" of his investigation. She sounded nervous over the phone, her voice taut with hesitation, but Max had assured her that any information she provided would be kept confidential. Now, as she ushered him into a small conference room down the hall from Lawson's office, Max could sense her anxiety in the quick, glancing looks she shot over her shoulder.

"Thank you for meeting with me, Detective," Carla said, her voice barely above a whisper as she took a seat across from him. She looked younger than he'd expected, probably in her early thirties, with sharp eyes that darted around the room as if making sure no one was eavesdropping.

"I appreciate you reaching out," Max replied, keeping his tone calm to put her at ease. "You mentioned you had information about Emily. Can you tell me what's going on?"

Carla bit her lip, her fingers nervously tapping on the edge of the table. "Emily... she was a brilliant girl. Strong-willed. But she was also... complicated. And, well, there are some things about her that not everyone knew."

Max leaned forward, giving her his full attention. "What kind of things?"

Carla's gaze shifted to the door before she spoke, lowering her voice even further. "Emily was... involved with someone. A man.

Someone she was very close to, but she didn't want anyone in her father's office to know about it."

"Who?" Max asked, his curiosity piqued.

"Marcus Dalton," Carla whispered, her eyes flashing with something between worry and relief. "He's a city councilman and a vocal critic of the senator. They've clashed on just about every issue, especially recently. But Emily..." Carla hesitated, as if she were betraying her friend by speaking of this. "Emily was drawn to him. They were... romantically involved."

Max's brows furrowed as he absorbed this information. "Emily was seeing one of her father's biggest political opponents? How long has this been going on?"

Carla sighed, her shoulders slumping. "Months, maybe longer. She kept it very secret, only confiding in a few people. She knew that if her father found out, it would create a scandal. Senator Lawson would never have approved."

The pieces began to fall into place. Max could see how Emily, fiercely independent and morally driven, would have been drawn to someone like Marcus Dalton. But the implications of her relationship with him went deeper than personal choice. This relationship could have stirred up jealousy, resentment, or even danger, especially if someone else in her father's circle found out.

"Did her father know anything about this?" Max asked, watching Carla's expression closely.

Carla shook her head. "Not that I know of. Emily was careful to keep it hidden from him. She knew he'd see it as a betrayal."

Max jotted down notes, his mind racing with new possibilities. "Do you think this relationship might have put her in any danger?"

Carla nodded slowly, her face clouding with worry. "Emily... she was fearless, Detective. She thought she could handle anything.

But this wasn't just about romance for her. She was helping Marcus. She believed he represented real change for Dominion City, and I think... I think she might have shared things with him, information about her father's allies and the people surrounding him. People with connections to The Sovereigns."

Max's gaze sharpened. "You're saying she might have shared sensitive information with Marcus Dalton?"

Carla swallowed, nodding. "I don't know for sure, but Emily was passionate. She believed in exposing corruption, and she believed in Marcus. She might have been helping him with his campaign, trying to give him leverage against the people in her father's circle."

A weight settled over Max's chest. If Emily had been confiding in Marcus about her father's connections, particularly those related to The Sovereigns, it was entirely possible that the wrong person had found out and seen her as a liability. Her relationship with Marcus could have made her a target in ways she hadn't anticipated.

Max took a deep breath, processing this new revelation. "Do you think Marcus was genuinely interested in her, or was he just using her to get information?"

Carla's face softened, a hint of sadness in her eyes. "I don't think he was using her. From what I saw... he seemed to care about her. Emily was drawn to his vision, his desire for change, and he respected her for her ideals. But Marcus is ambitious, and he has a lot to gain by challenging the senator and his allies."

Max nodded, understanding the delicate balance between personal and political motives. "Thank you, Carla. This information helps more than you know. Is there anything else you can tell me?"

She hesitated, her fingers fidgeting with a bracelet on her wrist. "There's one more thing. A few weeks ago, I overheard Emily talking to someone on the phone. She sounded... upset, like she was warning him about something. I only caught part of the conversation, but I remember her saying, 'They're watching us. We have to be careful.'"

Max's stomach tightened. Emily had clearly been aware of the dangers, yet she'd continued on her path regardless. "Do you know who she was talking to?"

"No," Carla said, shaking her head. "But if I had to guess, it was Marcus. She would never have confided in anyone else about something like that."

Max thanked Carla and stood to leave, his mind racing with questions. This new information changed everything. If Emily had been romantically involved with Marcus Dalton, a man who stood directly opposed to her father's allies and potentially The Sovereigns, then she may have found herself tangled in a web of political agendas, personal rivalries, and dangerous secrets.

As Max left Senator Lawson's office building, he resolved to track down Marcus Dalton and question him directly. He needed to know the full extent of Marcus's involvement in Emily's life—and in her investigation. If Marcus had been using Emily to gain information about her father's connections, then he might have known more than he'd let on, and he might still hold the key to understanding why she'd been taken.

The sun had dipped below the skyline, casting Dominion City in deepening shadows as Max headed back toward his car. Emily had been caught between two worlds—the world of her father's power and the promise of change that Marcus represented. But as Max considered the complexity of her connections, he realized that her trust in Marcus might have cost her more than she'd ever anticipated.

He climbed into his car, his resolve hardening. He would find Marcus Dalton and get answers, whatever it took. And if Marcus knew anything about The Sovereigns or the secrets, they were so desperate to protect, then Max was prepared to unravel the truth, one dangerous lead at a time.

Max returned to the police headquarters that evening, his thoughts heavy with the implications of Emily's relationship with Marcus Dalton. The revelation introduced new motives that could turn the investigation in an entirely different direction. As he walked down the hall toward the main briefing room, he was met by Adrian Cross, who appeared to be waiting for him, arms crossed and a look of smug satisfaction on his face.

"Carter," Adrian said, his tone oozing confidence, "I've got something that might interest you. Or maybe it'll just show you who's one step ahead on this case."

Max barely managed to hold back a sigh. He could already tell Adrian had something to prove, and his rival's eagerness to flaunt his "breakthrough" irritated him. But if Adrian had found something relevant, Max couldn't ignore it.

"All right, Cross," Max replied, keeping his voice even. "What did you find?"

Adrian smirked, holding up a file with a theatrical flourish before he flipped it open. "Turns out your missing girl wasn't quite the innocent crusader everyone thought. Emily Lawson was involved with none other than Marcus Dalton. She wasn't just dating him—she was feeding him information. Dirty secrets from her father's office."

Max clenched his jaw, realizing that Adrian had reached the same conclusion through his own investigation. "I'm aware of their relationship, Cross," he said, keeping his tone neutral. "And it's a lead worth following. But it doesn't automatically make Dalton a suspect."

Adrian's smirk widened. "Doesn't it, though? Let's think about this for a moment. Dalton's a politician with big ambitions, and he's got every reason to make Lawson look bad. Maybe he convinced Emily to dig up dirt for him, and when she got in too deep, he decided to cut ties. Or maybe he realized she'd become a liability and decided to get rid of her altogether."

Max resisted the urge to roll his eyes. "That's a big leap, Cross. We don't have any evidence that Marcus was trying to harm her. If anything, Emily was acting independently. She had her own reasons for investigating her father's allies."

Adrian gave a dismissive wave. "Come on, Carter. You're being naïve. Dalton's got motive written all over him. He's got the ambition, he's got the means, and he had access to her father's network through Emily. It all fits too perfectly to ignore."

Max shook his head, his irritation simmering beneath the surface. "And how do you know you're not walking into a setup? The Sovereigns know we're onto them. They've been planting misleads from the beginning. If they wanted us to think Dalton was the culprit, they'd make sure all the evidence pointed in his direction."

"Or maybe you're just too cautious, Carter," Adrian countered, a gleam in his eye. "This case needs someone willing to take risks. You're too busy second-guessing to see the obvious answer right in front of you."

SHADOWS OF DOMINION CITY

Max's patience wore thin as Adrian's arrogance bled into every word. He understood the pressure to solve this case, but Adrian's eagerness to cut corners threatened to derail everything they'd uncovered.

"So, you think pinning this on Dalton will wrap everything up nice and clean?" Max asked, his voice calm but challenging. "What happens if you're wrong, Cross? What if you let the real players slip through because you were too busy grandstanding?"

Adrian's face darkened, his smirk fading. "Don't lecture me, Carter. This isn't about grandstanding—it's about results. I get things done. I'm not here to waste time chasing shadows."

Max squared his shoulders, refusing to back down. "And I'm not here to jeopardize the case by jumping to conclusions. Emily's connection to Dalton is only one part of the picture. If we narrow our focus too soon, we risk overlooking the bigger players."

Adrian scoffed. "The bigger players, huh? You mean the 'all-powerful Sovereigns'? You're starting to sound like a conspiracy theorist."

Max's eyes flashed with irritation. "The Sovereigns aren't a theory, Cross. We have symbols, hidden connections, and people who were in Emily's life who keep disappearing. The Sovereigns are real, and if you'd stop trying to take shortcuts, maybe you'd see that."

Adrian's jaw tightened, his gaze hardening. "Fine. You chase your cult theory, Carter. But I'll be following real leads. I'm taking a team to Marcus Dalton's office tonight. I want to be there when he cracks and tells us why he had Emily digging up secrets."

Max shook his head, unable to hide his frustration. "You're putting all your faith in one lead, Cross. That's reckless."

Adrian sneered; his confidence unwavering. "Reckless or not, I'll get answers. Don't worry—I'll let you know what we find out. Assuming there's anything left to tell."

With that, Adrian brushed past Max and strode down the hallway, leaving Max alone in the briefing room. Max clenched his fists, taking a slow, measured breath to steady himself. Adrian's determination to pursue Marcus as a primary suspect wasn't just short-sighted—it was dangerous. If the real perpetrators were indeed manipulating the investigation, then Adrian's single-minded focus could lead them straight into a trap.

Max took a moment to collect his thoughts. Adrian's approach might appeal to officials eager for a quick resolution, but Max knew that cases like this didn't resolve cleanly. The truth was buried beneath layers of deception, and those who pursued it recklessly were likely to end up as casualties.

Determined to stay the course, Max returned to his desk, reviewing Emily's notes and re-examining the network of connections she had uncovered. If Marcus was innocent, then someone else close to Emily or her father was pulling strings to throw them off the scent. And if The Sovereigns were as powerful as he suspected, then Marcus was likely just one pawn in a much larger game.

Max reached for his phone and dialed a contact who'd previously provided him with information about The Sovereigns. He needed to know who else Emily might have uncovered, and he needed it soon. This was no longer just about finding Emily. It was about dismantling the network that held Dominion City in its grasp—a network that Adrian was too blind to see.

Late that night, a chilling call came through Max's phone, yanking him from his research on Emily's notes. The voice on the other end was tense, grim, and unmistakably familiar—it was an officer from the downtown precinct.

"Detective Carter, we need you down here," the officer said. "There's been... an incident. We've got a body."

Max's pulse quickened. "Who?"

"Jake Morrison," the officer replied, his voice laced with apprehension. "Emily Lawson's ex-boyfriend. Found him dead outside his apartment complex. Looks like it was staged as a mugging, but something's off."

Max's gut twisted. Jake Morrison had been one of Emily's closest connections, and he'd been uneasy during his previous interview with Max. Now, only days later, he was dead. It was too convenient to be a coincidence, too staged to be random.

"I'm on my way," Max replied, grabbing his coat and heading out into the chilly night air.

Max arrived at the scene to find the alleyway outside Jake's upscale apartment cordoned off with yellow tape, police officers standing guard around the dimly lit area. The alley was lined with dumpsters and strewn with scattered trash, a stark contrast to the luxury building towering above it. An ambulance waited nearby, its lights casting an eerie glow across the pavement as paramedics prepared to transport the body.

Max ducked under the tape and approached the crime scene, where an officer guided him to Jake's lifeless form. Jake lay slumped against the wall, his face pale and bruised, a look of shock frozen in his glassy eyes. His wallet was missing, and his watch was broken—a clear attempt to make it look like a robbery gone wrong. But as Max examined the scene more closely, subtle details betrayed the true nature of the crime.

The angle of Jake's body, the faint markings around his neck, the way his jacket was neatly arranged—it all suggested a deliberate hand, not the chaos of a mugging. Whoever had killed him had taken the time to carefully position him, ensuring that it would appear accidental to anyone who wasn't looking too closely.

Max knelt down, examining the bruises on Jake's face and the small cuts on his knuckles. There had been a struggle, but the killer had been skilled, overpowering him without leaving any obvious evidence. Max's fingers brushed against a small piece of torn fabric near Jake's shoulder, a remnant of dark cloth that didn't match Jake's clothing. He pocketed it, intending to have it analyzed.

One of the officers cleared his throat, looking nervously toward Max. "Sir, we found something else. A phone, smashed a few feet from the body. We think it's Jake's."

Max followed the officer's gesture to a cracked cell phone lying on the ground nearby. The screen was shattered, but it appeared intact enough to retrieve data. He motioned to the forensics team to secure it for examination, his mind already piecing together the possibilities.

As he stood, he heard familiar footsteps approaching behind him. Adrian Cross, dressed sharply as always, arrived on the scene, his face a mask of irritation mixed with intrigue.

"Well, Carter," Adrian said, crossing his arms as he surveyed the scene. "Looks like you were right about one thing—Jake Morrison's death isn't just a coincidence. But let me guess, you're about to spin this into another one of your cult theories."

Max met Adrian's gaze; his tone steady. "This isn't a theory, Cross. Jake knew something about Emily, something dangerous enough to get him killed. This wasn't a mugging—it was a warning. Someone wanted him silenced."

Adrian raised an eyebrow, his smirk fading. "You really think The Sovereigns would go to all this trouble just to take out her ex-boyfriend? Maybe he owed the wrong people money, or maybe he was into something shady. Not everything leads back to your invisible cult."

Max's patience was wearing thin, but he kept his voice calm. "Jake's death isn't about money or petty crime. It's a message. We both know he was connected to Emily. He was one of the few people she trusted, and she would have confided in him if she felt threatened."

Adrian scoffed, shaking his head. "So, what's your theory, then? That this is all some grand conspiracy orchestrated by shadowy figures in expensive suits? We have real suspects, Carter. People with real motives, not just myths and symbols."

Max clenched his jaw, forcing himself to stay focused. He couldn't let Adrian's skepticism derail him. "Listen to me, Cross. Whoever killed Jake wants us to think this is random. But look around—this crime scene is too carefully arranged. The person responsible wanted us to see it, to draw our own conclusions. And that means they're hiding something."

Adrian rolled his eyes, but Max noticed a flicker of doubt behind his bravado. "Fine. Say you're right. What do you suggest we do?"

"We start by finding out what Jake knew," Max replied, his tone firm. "We analyze his phone, dig into his recent calls, and see if there's any record of contact with Emily. And we take this lead seriously, even if it doesn't fit your picture-perfect narrative."

Adrian hesitated, then shrugged, clearly unwilling to concede but smart enough to follow through on Max's advice. "All right,

Carter. But don't expect me to go along with every crazy idea you come up with."

Max barely acknowledged the comment, already focused on his next steps. He motioned to the forensics team to examine Jake's body and gather any trace evidence, feeling a familiar surge of frustration as he sensed Adrian's doubt lingering behind him. Despite their conflicting methods, he knew they needed to work together if they were going to uncover the truth.

As the paramedics began to load Jake's body into the ambulance, Max felt a pang of guilt. Jake had been a flawed but genuine person, caught up in something he hadn't understood, something far bigger than he'd realized. And now, like Emily, he was gone.

"Detective Carter," one of the forensics technicians called, breaking through his thoughts. "We found this in his pocket."

The technician held up a small, crumpled piece of paper. Max took it carefully, unfolding it to reveal a single word scrawled in hurried handwriting: *Architect*.

Max's heart skipped a beat. The Architect—Emily's shadowy figure, the rumored leader of The Sovereigns, the person she'd feared most. Somehow, Jake had known about this figure too, and that knowledge had cost him his life.

"Architect?" Adrian repeated, glancing over Max's shoulder. "What is that? Some code name?"

Max folded the paper, slipping it into his pocket. "It's a lead," he said quietly, more to himself than to Adrian. "And one that just got a lot more real."

The gravity of the situation settled over him. The Architect wasn't just a figure in Emily's notes. He was real, dangerous, and clearly determined to eliminate anyone who got too close to his secrets. And now, Jake's death confirmed that Max was one step closer to a truth that The Sovereigns would kill to protect.

As he walked away from the crime scene, Max felt the weight of the case pressing down on him. Jake's death wasn't just another crime—it was a warning, a reminder that the path ahead was dark and treacherous. But no matter the cost, Max knew he wouldn't stop until he uncovered the truth, even if that meant going head-to-head with the most dangerous people in Dominion City.

Max returned to his office in the early hours, running on caffeine and determination. The investigation into Jake Morrison's death weighed heavily on his mind, and he'd hardly had time to process the slip of paper he'd found with the word *Architect* scrawled in Jake's handwriting. It was another clue leading to the heart of The Sovereigns, but it also raised troubling questions. Had Jake known who the Architect was, or had he simply been echoing Emily's fears?

As he sat reviewing notes, Max's phone buzzed with an alert from the department's digital forensics team. They had pulled a significant lead from the files Adrian had seized from Douglas Reyland's office earlier—a series of encrypted messages that Reyland had recently exchanged with someone identified only as "R.F." in the case file. According to the report, *R.F.* was allegedly a former Sovereign, now willing to help expose the cult. The messages suggested a meeting location, tonight, in the alleyway near the old Dominion Bank.

Max's gut reaction was caution. Reyland's ties to The Sovereigns made any information from his files suspect, and "R.F." could easily be a setup. But if there was even a chance that a former cult member wanted out and was willing to expose them, Max knew he had to follow the lead.

As the sun rose, Max prepared for the meeting, steeling himself for what could either be a breakthrough—or a dead end.

Later That Night

The Dominion Bank building loomed like a relic from another era, its weathered façade covered in ivy and shadows. The alley behind it was dark, save for the faint glow of a streetlamp casting a pool of light over damp cobblestones. Max waited, his back against the wall, watching for any sign of movement. The quietness of the street felt oppressive, and every sound seemed to amplify in the silence.

Max checked his watch. The message had set the meeting time for midnight, but as the minutes ticked past, his doubts grew. If this meeting was a setup, it was unlikely anyone would show. And if "R.F." was genuine, they might have decided it was too dangerous to go through with the meeting.

Suddenly, footsteps echoed down the alley. Max tensed, his hand instinctively moving toward his weapon. He squinted into the shadows, his eyes tracking a figure who emerged from the darkness, hooded and moving cautiously. The figure stopped just out of the streetlamp's glow; their face obscured.

"R.F.?" Max called, keeping his voice low and calm.

The figure shifted, their silhouette tense. "Are you alone?" a rough voice asked, barely a whisper.

"Yes. But I don't have time for games," Max replied, edging closer. "If you have information about The Sovereigns, now's the time to share it."

The figure hesitated, looking over their shoulder, and Max felt a surge of hope. But before they could respond, a flash of headlights swept across the alley, illuminating them both. In that instant, the figure's hand shot up, shielding their face, and Max saw a look of pure panic in their eyes.

"Get out of here!" the figure hissed, stepping backward into the shadows. But it was too late—the car pulled into the alley, its headlights blinding, and the sound of an engine revving filled the air. The figure took off in a sprint, vanishing into the maze of side streets before Max could react.

Max barely had time to draw his weapon before he heard a voice call out from the car.

"Carter! What the heck are you doing here?"

Adrian Cross climbed out of the driver's seat; his face set in an exasperated glare. Max lowered his weapon, his heart pounding, as Adrian approached him, a smug look of disbelief on his face.

"Waiting for a ghost?" Adrian asked, his tone dripping with sarcasm.

Max scowled, holstering his weapon. "This wasn't your lead, Cross. What are you doing here?"

Adrian leaned against his car, crossing his arms. "Funny thing about encrypted messages—turns out I can read too. When I saw the files from Reyland's office, I figured I'd follow up. Looks like I saved you from wasting your night on a wild goose chase."

Max's frustration boiled over. "You don't get it, do you? That was a potential informant—a Sovereign who might've turned on the cult. And thanks to your dramatic entrance, they're gone."

Adrian shrugged, clearly unimpressed. "If they really wanted to help, they'd have stuck around. But my guess? They saw you and realized you weren't going to fall for whatever story they cooked up. Just another distraction."

Max clenched his fists, struggling to stay calm. "Or maybe they actually had information, and they were scared of being caught."

Adrian's expression grew smug, his eyes narrowing. "You're in over your head, Carter. You're so obsessed with your conspiracy theories that you're willing to chase after phantoms. Meanwhile, I'm following real leads."

Max turned to face him; his voice icy. "Real leads? The only reason we're this close to the truth is because I didn't let go of those so-called conspiracy theories. Emily's disappearance, Jake's death—they're connected. And if you keep dismissing these leads, you're putting this entire case in jeopardy."

Adrian's expression hardened. "Let me make this clear, Carter. You may think you're onto something big, but you're only going to get people hurt by playing hero. There's a reason I was assigned to this case."

Max held Adrian's gaze; his resolve unwavering. "People are already getting hurt, Cross. And as long as I'm on this case, I'm going to pursue every lead, whether you approve or not."

Adrian let out a short laugh, his eyes glinting with disdain. "Fine. Waste your time with your imaginary informants. Just remember—you're not the only detective on this case, and I'm not going to let you get in my way."

With that, Adrian turned on his heel, leaving Max standing alone in the alley, the sound of the engine fading as Adrian drove away. Max took a steadying breath, looking down the dark alley where his informant had disappeared. If this had been a trap, The Sovereigns had succeeded in creating a perfectly orchestrated diversion. But if "R.F." was real, then Max had just lost his only direct link to The Sovereigns.

Back in his office, Max reviewed the file once more, noting that the messages between Reyland and "R.F." were vague, almost too vague. He began to suspect that the entire tip about a rogue cult member might have been deliberately planted in Reyland's files as a decoy, a way to lure Max off course and frustrate his progress. The Sovereigns had proven themselves ruthless and calculating, and Max couldn't shake the feeling that he was being watched, his every move anticipated.

He stared at his desk, a slow realization dawning on him. The Sovereigns weren't just one step ahead—they were weaving a complex web of lies, using red herrings to keep him and Adrian occupied, buying themselves time to cover their tracks. The closer Max got, the more obstacles they threw in his way, like a deadly game of cat and mouse.

As he pocketed the file, Max felt the weight of the night's events settle over him. The Sovereigns were no longer just a shadowy presence—they were actively manipulating his investigation, ensuring that every path he took was littered with traps and dead ends. But if they thought he'd give up now, they were wrong. He was more determined than ever to find Emily and expose the people behind her disappearance, no matter how deep he had to dig.

In the back of his mind, the image of the symbol—the three interlocking circles—lingered like a silent reminder. The Architect and The Sovereigns had woven a web that spanned the entire city, and he was only beginning to see the scale of their reach. But Max knew one thing for certain: he wasn't going to let them win.

He grabbed his coat and headed out, determined to keep searching. The hunt for the truth had only just begun, and he was prepared to face whatever lay in the shadows.

Chapter 4: The Cult Unveiled

Max's office was dimly lit, the feeling of fatigue pressing on him after another night of restless research. He had gone over Emily's notes, the clues surrounding Jake's death, and every fragment of information he had on The Sovereigns. Yet, the puzzle felt unsolvable—pieces scattered too widely to form a clear picture. He needed something substantial, something that would link the cult to a motive for Emily's kidnapping and to the city's tangled web of power.

As he massaged his temples, he was interrupted by a quiet knock on his door. He looked up to see Sarah Blane, the investigative journalist, standing in the doorway. She looked drained, her face pale, and her hands clutched a slim folder to her chest.

"Detective Carter," she said in a hushed voice, stepping into the office. "I have something. I wasn't sure I should bring it to you... but I knew Emily would want me to."

Max stood, motioning for her to sit as he took the folder from her hands. "Sarah, thank you for coming in. You did the right thing." He opened the folder and was greeted with a mix of photographs, handwritten notes, and old newspaper clippings, all loosely bound together. Sarah had carefully annotated each document with sticky notes, her cursive handwriting guiding him through each piece.

"These are... some of the things Emily had been researching," Sarah explained, her voice trembling slightly. "I found them in her apartment. She had been working tirelessly, connecting people, places, and... she kept mentioning her father's name."

Max flipped through the documents, his eyes scanning over images of Dominion City's elite at private events, dinners, and gatherings. Among the faces, he saw familiar names: businessmen, politicians, council members. Some were people he had crossed paths with during his time on the force. And then he found one photograph that sent a chill down his spine—a gathering in a grand, candle-lit room where men and women were dressed in formal attire, their faces partially obscured by shadow. In the middle of the group, smiling, was Senator Robert Lawson.

Max's brow furrowed. "Emily's father... was he involved with them?"

Sarah nodded, her expression tense. "I think so. Emily always looked up to him, but she started finding things she couldn't ignore—financial records, correspondences, even coded messages. She'd confided in me that he wasn't just aware of The Sovereigns... he was part of them. Or, at least, connected to people who were."

Max's jaw tightened as he examined a ledger from among the documents. It was a financial record showing a series of transactions from government accounts to anonymous shell corporations. The amounts were significant, and every payment was carefully disguised, flowing through layers of bogus companies to ensure secrecy. Each company, however, was subtly linked to a single entity—one that Max recognized as a front for The Sovereigns.

"These transactions..." he murmured, tracing the lines on the ledger. "They're a trail of kickbacks, donations funneled to people close to Lawson."

Sarah leaned forward, nodding. "Emily believed these were payments for loyalty, a kind of bribery to keep people in line. The

Sovereigns reward those who help them, but they punish anyone who tries to expose them."

As Max looked back through the photos, his eyes narrowed at the detail. In several of the images, he saw men and women wearing a familiar emblem—a small pendant with three interlocking circles, the same symbol he had seen etched near the scene of Emily's kidnapping and worn by the man in the surveillance photos. The more he looked, the clearer the pattern became. The people wearing the pendant appeared to gravitate toward one another, each exchange whispered, each handshake quick and discreet. They seemed to share an unspoken bond, a silent understanding that no one outside their circle would recognize.

"This isn't just about Emily's father, is it?" Max asked, his voice barely above a whisper. "It's the whole city."

Sarah's gaze met his, and her eyes held a deep, lingering sadness. "It's more than just the city, Max. The Sovereigns are a network that spans beyond Dominion City. But here... here is where they hold the most power. They've infiltrated every corner of influence—the police, the government, business. They keep each other protected, and they thrive by staying hidden."

Max clenched his fists as he thought of Emily, a young woman brave enough to investigate forces far beyond her reach. Her desire to seek truth and justice had placed her in the line of fire, and now, her life—and the lives of others—were in peril because of it.

"Sarah," he said, his tone grave, "did Emily ever talk about how far her father was willing to go to protect these people? Was he complicit in what they were doing?"

Sarah hesitated, her fingers twisting nervously in her lap. "She never said he was complicit. But she did think he was torn. Emily said that he'd built a career based on certain alliances, and some of those alliances were with Sovereigns. She thought that... maybe he was in too deep, that he knew things he couldn't unlearn."

Max took a deep breath, staring at a photograph of Lawson shaking hands with a known Sovereign financier. "Maybe Lawson didn't agree with everything they did, but he chose to stay involved for the sake of his career," Max muttered. "That makes him complicit, whether he sees it or not."

As Max continued leafing through the file, he came across another document that caught his attention—a handwritten note from Emily, scribbled hastily and almost frantic in tone. It read, *"It all leads back to the Architect. He holds their loyalty, their secrets. He knows everything, and they follow him without question."*

Sarah pointed to the note. "The Architect. Emily mentioned him once or twice to me. She said he was the leader, the one who held the city's darkest secrets. Emily thought that if she could expose him, the entire network would unravel."

Max's pulse quickened. The Architect—this mysterious figure had been lurking in the shadows of his investigation, leaving clues and hints but never revealing his identity. If Emily had been right, then finding the Architect was the only way to dismantle The Sovereigns and uncover the truth behind her disappearance.

Max looked back at Sarah, his mind whirring. "Did she have any leads on who the Architect might be?"

Sarah shook her head, a look of frustration crossing her face. "No. She only said that the Architect was careful, always careful. She thought he was someone powerful, someone who could hide in plain sight."

Max felt the weight of this revelation settle over him. The Architect wasn't just a name in Emily's notes. He was a real figure, a dangerous one, and he was closer than anyone realized.

Max took Sarah's hands, his grip firm but gentle. "Sarah, thank you. You've done more than you know by bringing me this."

Sarah nodded, giving him a tired smile. "Emily was my friend. She didn't deserve any of this."

Max's resolve strengthened as he closed the file and rose from his desk. The Sovereigns' web of influence was more insidious than he'd imagined, and it spanned the highest levels of power in Dominion City. But with the evidence Sarah had brought him, he was closer than ever to exposing the truth.

The clock on the wall struck midnight, but Max knew he couldn't rest. Not when Dominion City's most powerful players were still moving behind the scenes, hiding in the shadows and masking their crimes. Emily had believed in truth and justice, and Max would honor her memory by uncovering the secrets she had fought so hard to expose.

As Sarah left, Max sat back in his chair, staring at the folder in front of him. Somewhere in these papers was the key to finding the Architect and bringing down The Sovereigns. He just needed to find it before they silenced him too.

The waterfront was bathed in the faint orange glow of early evening as Max Carter approached the narrow alley by the river where his informant had arranged to meet him. The air was thick with the scent of brine and decay, the distant hum of traffic muted against the slap of water against the shore. His contact, a low-level member of The Sovereigns who had hinted at having vital information about the cult's inner workings, had insisted on this secluded location. Max's instincts told him to stay alert; every interaction involving The Sovereigns was tinged with risk.

As he neared the agreed-upon location, Max spotted a small crowd gathered along the riverbank, murmuring to one another in hushed voices. His heart sank as he noticed the flash of red-and-blue police lights illuminating the water, casting eerie reflections that shimmered over the quiet ripples.

Max approached an officer standing guard, his badge on display as he asked, "What happened here?"

The officer's face darkened. "Looks like we got a drowning victim, Detective. Just pulled him from the river. ID'd as a Danny Keene."

Max's breath hitched. Danny Keene—his informant. Max's eyes flickered toward the river, where two officers were hoisting a body bag onto the embankment. His jaw tightened, and a knot of anger twisted in his stomach. Keene had known the risks of coming forward, yet he'd agreed to talk. And now he was dead.

"Are we certain it was an accident?" Max asked, though he already sensed the answer.

The officer shrugged. "Found no signs of struggle, but the guy was a known addict, wasn't he? Could've just taken a bad turn, fallen in, and couldn't get out."

Max clenched his fists, pushing down his frustration. He knew Danny Keene had a rough past, but Danny's death, on the very night he was set to provide critical information, was too much of a coincidence. Yet, the officer's dismissive tone suggested no one else saw it that way.

A familiar voice spoke up behind him, dripping with skepticism. "Let me guess, Carter. You're about to spin this into another grand conspiracy?"

Max turned to see Adrian Cross approaching; his smirk barely concealed. Adrian took one look at the scene, his expression shifting from curiosity to contempt as he processed the situation.

"Let me save you some time," Adrian continued, crossing his arms. "Keene's death is a tragic accident, Carter. You're letting your paranoia get the better of you."

Max shot Adrian a hard look. "This wasn't an accident, Cross. Keene knew things. Things that could expose The Sovereigns, and now he's dead. How convenient."

Adrian sighed, waving a dismissive hand. "Oh, come on. Keene was a junkie and a petty crook. These types end up dead every day, either from their habits or their bad decisions. Maybe he was out of his mind on something, took a stumble, and that was that."

Max felt his patience erode, but he forced himself to keep his tone steady. "He was afraid, Adrian. Afraid of The Sovereigns, and for good reason. He was ready to talk. He'd been living in fear, but he knew he couldn't keep hiding. The night he agrees to meet me, he winds up dead? It's not a coincidence."

Adrian rolled his eyes, folding his arms across his chest. "You see conspiracy where there's nothing, Carter. Keene was just a low-life looking to make a quick deal. You're wasting time following ghosts."

Max's anger simmered, his hands clenching as he fought to keep control. "And you're too willing to write everything off as coincidence. We have too many 'accidents' piling up around this case, too many people disappearing or dying the moment, they get close to The Sovereigns. If you don't see the pattern, you're choosing not to."

Adrian scoffed, a smirk playing on his lips. "The only pattern I see is you chasing shadows. You're letting obsession blind you, Carter. Maybe take a step back before you start seeing cult symbols in your coffee."

SHADOWS OF DOMINION CITY

The barb stung, but Max didn't flinch. He stepped closer, meeting Adrian's gaze with steely resolve. "You know what's funny, Cross? You're so quick to mock me, but deep down, I think you're afraid. You know there's something bigger here, something that doesn't fit into your neat little boxes. You'd rather dismiss it than admit you're out of your depth."

Adrian's smirk vanished, replaced by a flicker of irritation. "Watch it, Carter. Don't forget I outrank you."

Max didn't back down. "Go ahead. Pull rank if that makes you feel in control. But I'll keep following the truth, whether or not it fits your story."

For a tense moment, they stood there, locked in silent standoff, the weight of their rivalry pressing down like a storm ready to break. Finally, Adrian broke eye contact, a sneer curling his lip as he turned away.

"Waste your time if you want, Carter. I'll be focused on finding real leads."

With that, Adrian walked off, leaving Max alone by the riverbank. Max took a steadying breath, his anger fading as he turned back toward the police officers who were gathering evidence. He knew he couldn't expect Adrian's help; he would have to handle this investigation alone.

Max took a closer look at the scene, scanning for anything out of place. He noticed something glinting just a few feet from where Keene's body had been found—a metal charm, barely visible beneath a cluster of weeds along the riverbank. He bent down, carefully plucking it up. It was a small pendant shaped like three interlocking circles, the same symbol that haunted his investigation from the beginning. The Sovereigns' mark.

The charm was cold in his hand, the weight of it reinforcing his suspicions. Whoever killed Danny Keene had left this here, either as a warning or a message. It was an eerie reminder that The Sovereigns were always watching, controlling every piece of the puzzle.

The sound of soft footsteps caught his attention, and Max looked up to see Sarah Blane approaching, her face drawn with worry. She had likely heard about Keene's death through her network of contacts and had come to check on the scene.

"Max," she whispered, her eyes widening when she noticed the pendant in his hand. "They... they did this, didn't they?"

Max nodded, a grim determination settling over him. "Keene was ready to talk. He wanted out. They couldn't risk him exposing them."

Sarah's face paled as she glanced at the river, shivering as if chilled. "This won't stop, will it? They'll keep killing, keep hiding in the shadows. I don't think Emily ever knew how far they would go."

Max put a reassuring hand on her shoulder, feeling the urgency of the moment pressing down on him. "I'll find them, Sarah. And I'll bring them down, no matter how far I have to go."

She nodded, her expression a mixture of fear and hope. "Be careful, Max. The closer you get, the more dangerous this becomes."

Max understood her fear. The Sovereigns were a force that thrived on secrecy, and anyone who threatened that secrecy was marked. But he also knew he couldn't turn back now. With Keene's death, they'd sent a clear message. They would stop at nothing to protect their control over Dominion City.

Max slipped the pendant into an evidence bag, his mind racing. He needed to look deeper into the records Sarah had provided, dig into the financial ledgers, the photographs of the city's elite. Somewhere in that evidence was the key to unraveling the Sovereigns' network, to exposing their influence and finally learning the truth about what had happened to Emily.

As he left the scene, Max glanced back one last time, a surge of resolve flooding his veins. The Sovereigns had tried to silence him through fear, intimidation, and deception, but their tactics only fueled his drive to see this case through.

They wanted him to stop, but Max had no intention of letting their web of lies hold him back. He was closing in, and no number of red herrings or false leads would keep him from uncovering the truth.

Max spent the following hours poring over Sarah's documents, piecing together fragments of Emily's notes and analyzing everything he had learned so far about The Sovereigns. Each detail hinted at something larger and more sinister—an event that Emily had feared, a ritual she had hinted might take place soon. Max's gut told him that Emily's disappearance and The Sovereigns' plans were connected by a ticking clock.

By midnight, Max had found the missing link: an upcoming political summit known as the Dominion Summit, an annual event attended by the city's highest-ranking officials, prominent business leaders, and select members of law enforcement. The summit was a formal celebration of Dominion City's "progress," but Emily's notes suggested that this event was a front—a cover for The Sovereigns to gather, conduct private meetings, and perform a ritual that bonded members to their cause.

Max leaned back in his chair, the weight of his discovery sinking in. If The Sovereigns were planning to meet during the Dominion Summit, it meant that Emily's investigation had likely uncovered something about this ritual. And if she had gotten too close to the truth, they may have taken her to prevent her from exposing them.

He felt a chill run down his spine as he thought back to Keene's death, Jake's murder, and the carefully placed red herrings designed to throw him off course. The Sovereigns had been operating in the shadows for years, orchestrating their moves to keep their secrets safe. But now, they were coming together for something more significant—something they wanted to hide.

The Next Day

Max arrived at police headquarters early, greeted by the usual buzz of officers moving through the hallways. He was heading toward his office when he spotted Adrian Cross at the far end of the hall, talking with a few other detectives. Adrian's face lit up with that familiar smug look as he caught sight of Max.

"Morning, Carter," Adrian called, his voice laced with sarcasm. "You look exhausted. Too many late nights chasing after imaginary cults?"

Max ignored the jab, but his patience with Adrian had worn thin. "I don't have time for games, Cross. I'm here to discuss the Dominion Summit."

Adrian raised an eyebrow, his expression turning incredulous. "The summit? That's a political gala, Carter. Champagne, handshakes, and speeches. If you're thinking there's some grand conspiracy behind it, I suggest you get some sleep."

Max took a deep breath, keeping his tone steady. "Listen to me, Adrian. Emily was investigating The Sovereigns, and her notes indicate that the summit is more than just a gala. She believed there was a ritual tied to it, something involving the city's most powerful figures."

Adrian scoffed, crossing his arms. "A ritual? You're making it sound like a Halloween ghost story. Look, Carter, if you want to spin your wheels on this, go right ahead. But I have real leads to follow."

Max clenched his fists, struggling to stay calm. "This is serious, Cross. Emily uncovered connections between The Sovereigns and high-ranking officials. If they're meeting at the summit, then her disappearance is tied to whatever they're planning."

Adrian shook his head, his expression dismissive. "There's no proof, Carter. Just your paranoia and some scribbled notes. You want to believe there's a cult meeting under the cover of a gala? Be my guest. But I'm not wasting resources on your theories."

Max felt his frustration boiling over. He knew he couldn't convince Adrian to take the threat seriously, and the more he argued, the more Adrian dismissed him. Max took a deep breath, holding back the urge to snap back. He didn't have time to waste on Adrian's skepticism. He needed to prepare.

Later That Evening: Dominion City Hall

As night fell, Max parked his car a few blocks from Dominion City Hall, where the summit was being held. The city's historic government building was aglow with lights, the grand facade lined with red carpets and velvet ropes. Guests in formal attire entered in droves, mingling outside and greeting one another as reporters took photos and recorded sound bites.

Max blended into the crowd, his gaze scanning the attendees, looking for anything out of place. Despite the formal atmosphere, he noticed small, telling details: familiar faces clustered in hushed conversations, council members meeting discreetly with private financiers, and subtle glances exchanged by those wearing the now-familiar pendant with the three interlocking circles.

As he moved closer, he spotted Councilman Paul Haynes—the same councilman who had been evasive during earlier questioning about Emily. Haynes was deep in conversation with Douglas Reyland, the businessman whose office had provided some of the earliest clues. They exchanged a nod, their expressions tense, as they slipped through a side door leading into a restricted area.

Max's heart pounded as he followed them from a distance, keeping to the shadows. The hallways were lined with gilded mirrors and marble busts of past city officials, the grandeur only amplifying the secrecy of the ritual taking place somewhere within the building's depths. He noticed several guests moving discreetly down a back hallway, including others he recognized from Emily's notes. Each of them wore the Sovereigns' pendant—a silent emblem of their allegiance.

After a series of twists and turns through narrow corridors, Max heard the low murmur of voices and faint candlelight flickering against the walls. He ducked behind a corner, observing as the group gathered in a hidden chamber, the room dimly lit by tall, wax-dripping candles arranged in a circular pattern. A raised platform at the center held a large, intricately carved wooden table with symbols etched into its surface—the same interlocking circles Max had seen so many times before.

He could barely make out the faces of those gathered, but their somber expressions and the intensity of the atmosphere made it clear that this was no ordinary meeting. One of the figures—a man cloaked in a dark robe with the pendant hanging prominently around his neck—stepped forward, raising his hands to command silence.

Max's breath hitched as he recognized the man's voice, deep and measured. It was Senator Lawson.

"Tonight, we reaffirm our unity," Lawson said, his voice reverberating through the chamber. "Tonight, we bind our fates to The Sovereigns. We gather not only to protect our interests but to preserve our power, our legacy, and our truth."

The crowd murmured their agreement, their voices rising like a chant, repeating phrases Max couldn't fully make out. He strained to listen, his skin prickling with dread as he realized that Emily had been right—the ritual was real, and her father was at the center of it.

A hand suddenly clamped down on his shoulder, and Max whipped around, instinctively reaching for his weapon. But he froze as he met the familiar gaze of Adrian Cross, who had a furious look on his face.

"What the heck are you doing here, Carter?" Adrian hissed, his eyes darting to the chamber. "Are you out of your mind?"

Max's pulse quickened as he struggled to keep his voice low. "They're performing a ritual, Adrian. Look for yourself—your councilman, your businessmen. They're all part of The Sovereigns. This is the proof you've been ignoring."

Adrian's expression shifted from anger to confusion, his skepticism fading as he glanced toward the room, taking in the scene. For a moment, his bravado crumbled, replaced by something close to fear.

"Carter, this is... this is insane," Adrian whispered, his voice barely audible. "But if you're right... if they really are involved in something like this..."

Max nodded, his gaze steady. "We have to get out of here. If they catch us, they won't hesitate to silence us."

Adrian's face tightened, and he finally seemed to grasp the gravity of their situation. Without another word, he turned, gesturing for Max to follow him down the hall. But just as they began to backtrack, a figure appeared at the end of the corridor, blocking their exit. It was one of Lawson's aides, his expression cold and knowing.

"Detectives," the aide said calmly, his voice laced with menace. "You're not on the guest list. I suggest you come with me."

Max and Adrian exchanged a glance, their tension palpable. They both knew that compliance was not an option.

In a split-second decision, Max broke into a sprint, pulling Adrian with him as they raced down the hallway, dodging past the aide and darting through a series of doors. Behind them, footsteps echoed, the sounds of more figures joining the chase.

They burst through an emergency exit, the cold night air slapping their faces as they stumbled out onto a side street, their hearts pounding. The city lights glittered in the distance, but neither man felt safe. Max knew they had narrowly escaped—tonight had been a stark reminder that they were no longer investigating from the outside. They had crossed a line, and The Sovereigns would not forgive it.

As they caught their breath, Adrian looked at Max, his face pale, a mixture of fear and respect in his eyes. "You were right, Carter. This goes deep. Too deep."

Max nodded, feeling the weight of his discovery settling over him. "It's only the beginning, Cross. But now, we know exactly what we're up against."

SHADOWS OF DOMINION CITY

They stood in silence, the enormity of their discovery sinking in. They had uncovered the ritual, exposed the players, and, for the first time, had undeniable proof of The Sovereigns' existence. But the cost of this knowledge was high—and they both knew that their lives would never be the same.

The dawn crept over Dominion City, casting pale light across the empty streets as Max and Adrian made their way back to headquarters. The events of the previous night weighed heavily on them both, the memories vivid and raw. They had seen The Sovereigns in action, witnessed their ritual, and now knew the truth that had been lurking in the shadows all along. But that truth had come with a price: their own safety was compromised.

In silence, they climbed the steps to the police precinct, the weight of their discovery settling over them. Neither man spoke as they reached Max's office. The dim morning light filtered through the blinds, casting long shadows across the tables. Adrian, still pale from the night's events, dropped into a chair and stared blankly at the wall. Max could tell that his rival was shaken, but he was too focused on the next steps to address it.

Max moved to his desk, pushing aside the remnants of his earlier research. He pulled out Emily's notes, laying them in front of him as he reviewed her descriptions of The Sovereigns, her careful documentation of their influence and her suspicions of a ritual tied to the city's elite. Emily had been right about everything—the network, the ritual, even her father's involvement.

Just then, Sarah Blane appeared at the doorway, her eyes wide with anxiety. She glanced at Adrian, noting his hollow expression, before turning to Max.

"Max," she said, her voice barely above a whisper. "There's something you need to see."

Max followed her gaze to the folder clutched tightly in her hands. She handed it over, and he opened it, his stomach sinking as he realized what it contained.

The folder held photographs, documents, and handwritten notes—all detailing key members of Dominion City's government and their covert connections to The Sovereigns. There were names, dates, and details that confirmed everything he'd witnessed. But one document in particular caught his eye: a list of government officials who had quietly funneled public funds into Sovereign-controlled accounts. And at the very top of the list, highlighted in bold, was the name Senator Robert Lawson.

"This was just sent to me anonymously," Sarah explained, her voice trembling. "Whoever sent this wanted to expose the truth. It's evidence, Max—evidence that could bring the whole network down."

Max glanced over at Adrian, who had shifted in his chair, his face pale but resolute. He didn't speak, but Max could see that he understood the weight of what they held. They were no longer just investigators—they were now the keepers of the evidence that could dismantle The Sovereigns.

But before Max could respond, a loud knock sounded at his door, and an officer stepped in, his face solemn. "Detectives, there's something you both need to see. It's urgent."

The officer led them down the hall to a side office where the precinct's captain stood waiting. He looked tense, his usual authoritative presence overshadowed by a palpable unease.

"What's going on, Captain?" Max asked, his instincts on high alert.

Without a word, the captain motioned for them to follow, leading them into his office. On his desk lay a single object that seemed innocuous at first—a small, polished wooden box, elegantly carved and set with the three interlocking circles of The Sovereigns' symbol. The captain gestured for them to open it.

Max exchanged a wary glance with Adrian before lifting the lid. Inside was a note, handwritten on fine paper, the edges charred as if to make the message clear: it was a warning. The message read, *"You were seen. Walk away, or you will lose everything."*

A chill ran down Max's spine as he processed the threat. The Sovereigns knew they had been at the ritual. They knew that Max and Adrian were onto them—and now they were issuing a final warning. The message was clear: if they continued, they would pay the ultimate price.

Adrian took a shaky breath, his face ashen. "They know... they know everything. They're watching us."

Max closed the box, his mind racing. For years, The Sovereigns had operated in the shadows, but now they were moving openly, daring him to continue. It was a high-stakes gambit, but Max knew that this message would only fuel his determination.

Just as they were about to leave the captain's office, a junior officer rushed in, holding another item wrapped in cloth. She glanced nervously at Max, then at Adrian, before carefully placing it on the captain's desk. The captain nodded, and she unwrapped it, revealing a photograph—a picture of Emily Lawson.

But it wasn't just any photo. Emily appeared pale and frail, sitting in a dimly lit room with her hands bound and her eyes staring directly into the camera, her expression a mixture of defiance and fear. On the back of the photo was another handwritten note: *"This is your last chance. The summit was only the beginning."*

Max felt the ground shift beneath him, his heart pounding in his chest. Emily was alive, but barely—and the photo was their way of taunting him, of letting him know she was just out of reach. The Sovereigns were flaunting their control, their ability to manipulate everyone around them, and this photo was their final warning.

Adrian stood beside him, silent but visibly shaken, his face betraying the horror of their discovery. They had come closer to finding Emily than ever, but this photo reminded them just how powerful and unreachable The Sovereigns truly were.

Max clenched his fists, his resolve hardening as he stared down at the image. They were taunting him, daring him to continue, but he wasn't going to back down. This was no longer just about exposing The Sovereigns or saving Emily—it was about bringing down the entire corrupt network that held Dominion City in its grip.

"We need to act fast," Max said, his voice steely, filled with purpose. "Emily's alive, and they're using her as leverage. But we're going to turn the tables. We have what we need to take them down."

Adrian nodded slowly; his skepticism finally broken. "I'm with you, Carter. Whatever it takes."

As they left the captain's office, the photograph of Emily burned in Max's mind. He knew the dangers that lay ahead, knew the risks, but he also knew that he wouldn't rest until The Sovereigns' grip on Dominion City was destroyed—and Emily was finally safe.

Chapter 5: Another Murder

The early morning sun barely penetrated the fog that hung over Dominion City's affluent Evergreen Heights district. Max Carter parked his car at the end of a long, winding driveway leading up to the grand mansion of Harold Wexler, one of the city's most influential lobbyists and a known associate of the city's most powerful elites. Wexler's connections and rumored influence in The Sovereigns had made him a prime suspect in Emily's disappearance, but Max hadn't expected to visit him under these circumstances.

As he stepped out of his car, Max noticed Adrian Cross pulling up alongside him. Adrian's expression was steely, his posture tense as he surveyed the mansion's imposing stone façade, guarded by two uniformed officers who looked visibly shaken. Word had already spread: a high-profile murder in Evergreen Heights wasn't just another case—it was an earthquake.

Inside, the mansion was eerily silent. Officers and forensic techs moved about quietly, some exchanging hushed whispers. One detective approached Max and Adrian as they entered, nodding grimly.

"He's in the study," the detective said, gesturing down the corridor. "It's... well, you'll see."

Max and Adrian exchanged a look before making their way down the hallway, which was lined with dark wood paneling and heavy oil paintings depicting scenes of battles and solemn men in somber colors. The decor gave off a sense of history and importance, a deliberate attempt to project an air of legacy and power.

They reached the study door, which had been left ajar. Inside, the scene was chilling: Harold Wexler sat slumped over an enormous oak desk, his once-dignified face now pale and lifeless, a thin line of blood marking his throat where a blade had sliced clean through. His eyes were still open, wide with terror, and his hands lay limp on the desk, as though he'd been frozen in a final moment of horror.

Max stepped into the room, feeling the weight of the scene settle over him. The walls were covered in dark wood, shelves lined with books on law and politics, their spines pristine and untouched. A large portrait of Wexler himself hung behind the desk, his painted eyes staring down as if judging everyone in the room.

"Brutal," Adrian murmured, his voice low as he surveyed the body. "Almost ceremonial."

Max nodded; his attention drawn to the symbols scrawled across the walls in blood. They were carefully drawn, deliberate—three interlocking circles, forming the now-familiar emblem of The Sovereigns. But there was something new added, an unusual phrase written in jagged letters beneath the symbol: *"Betrayed from within."*

The words sent a chill down Max's spine. This wasn't just a message—it was a statement, a warning that betrayal was brewing within The Sovereigns' ranks.

Max gestured to the writing. "Looks like someone within the cult wanted to make sure we saw this."

Adrian frowned, crossing his arms. "Or it's a setup. Someone trying to make it look like an inside job to throw us off."

Max stepped closer to the desk, studying Wexler's body for any clues. He noted that Wexler's hands were clutching the edge of his desk, his knuckles still faintly white as if he'd tried to brace himself. Nearby, an overturned glass lay on the floor, the remnants of a dark red liquid pooling across the expensive rug.

A crime scene investigator approached, handing Max a bagged item. "Detective, we found this tucked under his desk." Inside the bag was a small, bloodstained notebook, worn and weathered, as if it had been handled many times. Max carefully opened the first page, his heart pounding as he read the faint, scribbled words:

"The Architect knows all. Secrets are the currency. Trust is an illusion."

Max's jaw tightened. The Architect—the shadowy leader of The Sovereigns—was mentioned again. Every step of this investigation seemed to circle back to this figure, the one pulling the strings from behind the scenes, ensuring that The Sovereigns' influence remained unchallenged.

"Looks like Wexler knew he was in deep," Max murmured, showing the notebook to Adrian. "This wasn't just business. He was aware of the stakes, aware that his loyalty could be tested."

Adrian's gaze flickered over the words, a mix of interest and frustration in his eyes. "So, he was part of the cult, and maybe he wanted out. Or maybe he knew too much, and they took him out to keep him silent."

Max nodded, his mind racing with possibilities. "The message on the wall, the mention of betrayal—it could mean someone within The Sovereigns saw him as a threat. He might have crossed a line, broken one of their codes."

"Or he was about to reveal something," Adrian added, glancing around the room. "Something that could have exposed them."

Max felt the tension building as he processed the scene. The Sovereigns had shown their ruthlessness by killing one of their own, and the brutality of the crime spoke volumes about their desperation. This wasn't a quiet removal—it was a message to anyone within their ranks who dared to think about turning away.

As Max continued to examine the room, he noticed a faint trail of blood droplets leading from the desk toward a side door, partially hidden by a large tapestry. He motioned for Adrian to follow, and they approached the door, cautiously pushing it open.

The door led to a private study, smaller and more secluded than the main office. Unlike the pristine order of the main study, this room was cluttered, with papers strewn across the desk and maps pinned to the walls. Max scanned the documents, noting dates, locations, and cryptic symbols scrawled in the margins.

"What is all this?" Adrian asked, sifting through the papers.

Max's eyes landed on a document marked "Dominion Summit," with notes and initials indicating who had attended in years past. The initials included high-ranking officials, businessmen, and other influential figures—all linked by The Sovereigns' emblem. It was a meticulous list of attendees, people who had been groomed or coerced into supporting the cult's agenda.

A photo caught his eye, a recent image of Emily Lawson at one of the Sovereigns' gatherings, her expression tense and focused as she mingled with several people. She looked wary, her posture defensive, as if she'd known she was out of place.

Max felt a surge of anger and determination as he pocketed the photo. Emily's involvement wasn't just accidental—she had been pulled into The Sovereigns' orbit, and her knowledge of their secrets had likely led to her kidnapping.

Suddenly, a forensics tech stepped into the study, holding up a fingerprint sample. "Detectives, we've identified a partial print on the notebook cover. It's not Wexler's, and it doesn't belong to anyone in his household."

Max and Adrian exchanged a look. It was a small lead, but in a case as twisted as this, any detail was valuable. Max glanced back at the crime scene, the bloodied message on the wall echoing in his mind.

"Betrayed from within," he murmured. "Whoever left that message wanted us to know there's division in The Sovereigns. Someone's making a move, and it's causing fractures in their ranks."

Adrian's skepticism had faded, replaced by a grim understanding. "If they're willing to kill their own, then no one's safe."

Max nodded. The murder of Harold Wexler marked a turning point, shifting their investigation from a search for Emily to a battle with a cult that was slowly unraveling. The Sovereigns' unity was cracking, and now, Max and Adrian were closer to understanding the cult's inner workings than they had ever been.

As they exited the study, Max couldn't shake the feeling that they were being watched. Every step they took brought them closer to the truth—and closer to the danger that lay hidden within Dominion City's elite. But with Wexler's death, they had undeniable proof that The Sovereigns weren't just a secret society; they were a brutal, power-hungry force, willing to do anything to protect their hold on the city.

And now, they had left a trail of blood that Max intended to follow, no matter where it led.

Back at police headquarters, the briefing room was tense as detectives filed in, taking their seats around the long table. Max sat at the head, his mind still racing from the morning's crime scene. Harold Wexler's murder had raised the stakes to a new level, and everyone in the room seemed to understand that they were dealing with something far more sinister than a high-profile kidnapping.

Adrian entered a moment later, carrying a file packed with details on potential suspects. He dropped it onto the table and took a seat, his face set in a grim expression that reflected the severity of the situation.

"All right, listen up," Max began, his voice steady but urgent. "We're now dealing with a homicide. Wexler wasn't just killed—he was executed. And whoever did it wanted to send a message to The Sovereigns. The words 'Betrayed from within' were written in blood at the scene. This isn't just about Emily's disappearance anymore. We're looking at a power struggle within the cult."

A murmur of concern rippled through the room. Max waited until the tension settled, then turned to Adrian, who opened the file to a list of suspects.

"We've identified several individuals who had recent conflicts with Wexler or connections to The Sovereigns," Adrian said, his tone businesslike. "Let's start with the most obvious."

He flipped to the first page, which displayed a photo of Lucas Voss, a rival lobbyist and former business associate of Wexler's. The two had clashed over city contracts and political influence, and their relationship had soured over the past few years.

"Lucas Voss is a long-time competitor of Wexler's," Adrian explained. "They've been at odds for years, especially over city projects that Wexler had sway over. Voss had every reason to want Wexler out of the way, and he was seen in Dominion City the night of the murder. We haven't yet confirmed an alibi."

Max nodded, though his gut told him that Wexler's murder was deeper than a simple professional rivalry. "It's worth investigating. But we need to keep an open mind. Wexler's death doesn't feel like a business grudge—it feels personal, like someone within The Sovereigns wanted to make a statement."

Adrian gave a dismissive shrug but turned to the next page, which displayed a photo of Amanda Wexler, Harold's estranged daughter. She had returned to Dominion City recently after years of living abroad, following a public falling-out with her father that had made local headlines. Rumors circulated that she had never forgiven him for prioritizing his career over their family, and she'd been spotted in the city over the past few weeks.

"Amanda Wexler," Adrian continued. "Estranged daughter, back in town just weeks before her father's murder. She didn't hide her disdain for him, and it's possible she wanted revenge for the way he neglected her growing up."

Max studied Amanda's photo. She looked young, tough, her expression one of defiance. He didn't know if she'd be capable of something as brutal as her father's murder, but if she had been dragged into his world of influence and secrecy, she could have had a motive to lash out.

"Did she have any ties to The Sovereigns?" Max asked.

Adrian glanced down at his notes. "Nothing concrete, but some sources suggest that her father tried to groom her for involvement in the cult. She reportedly rejected it, which could have been a factor in their estrangement. But that's speculation at this point."

Max leaned back, considering the implications. Amanda might not have been directly involved in the cult, but she could have learned things from her father, secrets that would put her in danger or give her a reason to act out. If Wexler had pushed her to join the cult and she'd refused, that could have deepened their rift—and perhaps driven her to seek revenge.

"We'll need to talk to her," Max said, noting her name on his list. "Even if she didn't kill him, she might know more about his connection to The Sovereigns."

Adrian nodded and flipped to the next page, revealing a photo of Theo Raines, a lower-ranking member of The Sovereigns. He had been close to Wexler, often seen at his events and rumored to be one of Wexler's protégés. But according to recent reports, Theo had begun to distance himself from Wexler, voicing concerns about the cult's methods and goals.

"Theo Raines," Adrian said. "Wexler's protégé and close confidant—until recently. He's had a falling-out with the inner circle, and some say he's been critical of the way The Sovereigns have been handling their influence in the city."

Max's interest piqued. "So, Theo's a deserter?"

"Seems like it," Adrian replied. "Rumor is, he's grown disillusioned with The Sovereigns and was starting to pull away. That could make him a target for them, or he could have been trying to take control himself."

Max felt a flicker of hope. A member who was pulling away from the cult might hold valuable information. Theo could be their way into the inner workings of The Sovereigns, but he could also be a loose cannon if he felt threatened or betrayed.

"We'll need to bring Theo in and question him," Max said. "If he's breaking ties with the cult, he may be willing to talk. But we have to tread carefully—he could also be the killer, sending a message to Wexler and the rest of the cult."

Adrian looked up, his expression hardening. "And if Theo's a threat to The Sovereigns, that could mean he's a target. We'll need to act fast before someone silences him, too."

Max nodded, feeling the weight of their mission pressing down on him. They were looking for answers in a maze of power and secrecy, where every suspect was both a source of information and a potential danger. He glanced around the room, meeting the eyes of each officer, ensuring they understood the gravity of the case.

"Listen carefully," Max said, addressing the team. "Each of these suspects has ties to Wexler, either personally or professionally, and each one is connected to The Sovereigns in some way. This cult doesn't just kill randomly—they kill to control. Every lead we follow, every question we ask, could provoke them. We need to be cautious, thorough, and prepared for retaliation."

Adrian shifted in his seat, his eyes narrowing. "We should start with Voss. Rival or not, he's the one with the most obvious motive. I'll bring him in for questioning and see if I can rattle him."

Max gave a reluctant nod, though he was still more interested in Amanda and Theo. "Fine. But make sure you stay focused, Adrian. If this is about cult politics, Voss might just be a decoy."

Adrian smirked, a hint of his usual bravado returning. "Don't worry, Carter. I can handle a simple interrogation."

Max watched as Adrian rose, heading out to bring Voss in for questioning. Despite Adrian's confidence, Max couldn't shake the feeling that Voss was probably another wild goose chase—a convenient suspect thrown into the mix to distract them. The true answers likely lay deeper, in the tangled web of The Sovereigns' internal conflicts.

As the team dispersed, Max remained in the briefing room, reviewing the suspects' files once more. He was determined to get to the truth, but he knew that with each new suspect they questioned, they were only stirring the hornet's nest.

Amanda, Theo, and Voss each had motives and opportunities, but there was no clear path to follow. If The Sovereigns were indeed dealing with betrayal from within, then Wexler's murder was just the beginning. Whoever had killed him had sent a message, and Max feared they were far from finished.

With a final look at the suspects' photos, Max gathered his notes and prepared to question Amanda Wexler. She might be the key to understanding her father's involvement with The Sovereigns—and to unraveling the deadly secrets that had driven the cult to turn on its own.

The late afternoon sun cast long shadows across the walls of Harold Wexler's mansion as Max returned to the crime scene alone, hoping a quieter look might reveal something the initial sweep had missed. The mansion felt more ominous without the usual bustle of the police and forensic team; silence amplified every creak of the old floors as Max moved through the darkened halls.

He made his way back to Wexler's study, taking a deep breath before stepping inside. The room's grandeur was tainted by the eerie remnants of the murder—faint bloodstains still lingered on the polished wood floors and walls, along with the chilling message scrawled in Wexler's blood: *"Betrayed from within."* The phrase repeated in Max's mind like a sinister refrain, each word hinting at internal conflicts within The Sovereigns. If there was a power struggle brewing, then Wexler's murder was likely a calculated move, a warning to anyone else in the cult who dared to waver in loyalty.

Max began a slow, methodical search of the room, starting with the large, ornately carved desk where Wexler had been found slumped over. He sifted through drawers packed with correspondence, old business ledgers, and confidential memos, all meticulously organized. Wexler's handwriting was precise, each line neat, as if he had nothing to hide. But Max knew better.

As he reached the last drawer, his hand brushed against something unusual—a slight ridge beneath the felt lining. He pressed down, feeling for a latch, and with a quiet *click*, the lining lifted, revealing a hidden compartment. Inside, Max found a small stack of letters bound together with twine, the edges worn from handling. He carefully removed the bundle and opened the first letter.

The handwriting was slanted, hurried, and almost frantic—a stark contrast to Wexler's usual penmanship. The letter was unsigned, but a familiar phrase caught Max's eye: *"The Architect knows all."* Max's pulse quickened as he read further, piecing together fragments of sentences hinting at The Sovereigns' operations and their secret meetings.

"The Architect is growing more ruthless, pushing us beyond the boundaries we once agreed to... A reckoning is coming... Loyalty must be absolute, or consequences will be swift."

Max's breath caught as he absorbed the meaning behind the words. The Architect—the mysterious figure at the top of The Sovereigns' hierarchy—was enforcing control through fear and threats. Wexler must have known that anyone who questioned The Architect's authority was marked. His murder wasn't just punishment—it was an example.

Max placed the letter aside and opened another, quickly realizing that it contained sensitive financial information. The letter referenced substantial sums of money transferred to offshore accounts, each transaction cryptically linked to individuals who, by name alone, held powerful sway over Dominion City's infrastructure and policy decisions. Wexler had noted the initials of several high-profile figures involved, including one entry that made Max's heart race: R.L.

"Senator Robert Lawson," Max whispered to himself, the realization chilling him. Emily's father was more deeply entangled in The Sovereigns than he'd realized, tied to their financial network and, likely, their darkest dealings. This was no passing association. Lawson's presence in Wexler's files suggested that he was a major player, perhaps even the Architect himself or directly connected to him.

As Max sifted through the remaining letters, he found one addressed specifically to Wexler, the ink smeared in places as though it had been written in a hurry. The message was terse but carried a warning tone:

"Do not let dissent spread. Betrayal weakens us. The Architect's loyalty is absolute, and any who question it will pay."

Max felt a chill. This wasn't just a communication between associates—it was a direct threat from within The Sovereigns' inner circle. It confirmed what he had suspected all along: Wexler's death was orchestrated to send a message. But what had Wexler done to deserve such a fate?

Lost in thought, Max nearly missed a faint scratching sound from the back of the study. He turned, scanning the room, and noticed a second, smaller door half-hidden behind a tall bookshelf. He hadn't seen it earlier, likely because it blended into the dark wood paneling. He approached cautiously, easing the door open to find a dimly lit hallway leading to a private office, far smaller and less grand than the study. This room was cluttered with papers and maps, pinned in layers across the walls as if Wexler had been mapping out connections and tracking movements.

Max moved closer to the desk, studying the papers. Most were documents tied to Dominion City's infrastructure projects, but interspersed among them were handwritten notes in Wexler's urgent scrawl. A few notes stood out:

"Summit night, all players in place—only loyalty remains."

"Watch for signs of dissent among them; certain loyalties waver."

The last line Max read sent a shiver down his spine. *"An Architect's betrayal is the greatest risk. Trust no one, not even within."*

Max's mind raced. The words hinted at an internal split within The Sovereigns, as if even their highest-ranking members had begun to question The Architect's vision and methods. If Wexler had suspected betrayal, he might have tried to keep notes in this hidden room as leverage against his enemies.

His eyes shifted to a large map pinned to the wall, where red pins marked key locations around the city. Max traced his fingers along the pins, noting that each marked location corresponded to a Sovereigns member's residence or business. But one pin, in a different color, stood out—it was on a building he recognized from Emily's notes: the Dominion Club.

The Dominion Club, an exclusive venue for the city's elite, had hosted numerous Sovereign gatherings in recent months. Emily had speculated that the club served as a front for the cult's private meetings, a place where new initiates were vetted and deals were made under the guise of high-society networking events. This new connection felt like a key piece of the puzzle.

Max pulled out his phone and took pictures of the map and notes, determined to revisit the Dominion Club. Wexler's death had clearly stirred a hornet's nest, and if the Sovereigns had splintered into factions, then the club might be the site of their next showdown.

As he pocketed his phone, he spotted another document partially hidden beneath a stack of papers on the desk. The document was yellowed and faint, but the header made his heart skip: "The Day of Reckoning—Ritual of Renewal."

Max read through the details, his blood turning cold. It was a description of a Sovereign ritual, one that took place every decade and involved a "Renewal of Loyalty." According to the text, members reaffirmed their allegiance in a secret ceremony, one that bound them to silence under threat of death. The text described a chilling phrase: *"Sacrifices must be made to uphold the Sovereignty."*

The implications were clear. This ritual wasn't just symbolic—it was a binding pledge that silenced anyone who dared to break ranks. And if the upcoming Dominion Summit was tied to this ritual, then Wexler's death could have been the first in a series of purges. The Sovereigns were eliminating any sign of dissent before their renewal.

As Max finished reading, his phone buzzed. He answered it, recognizing Sarah Blane's voice on the other end. Her tone was hurried and panicked.

"Max, I just got a lead. One of my sources says they're planning something big at the Dominion Club tonight. They didn't have details, but they warned me not to go near the place. They said it's 'for members only.'"

Max's heart raced as he absorbed her words. "Did they mention anything about a ritual or loyalty renewal?"

Sarah hesitated. "Not in so many words, but... they said it was going to be a 'cleansing.' Max, whatever they're doing tonight, it's going to be dangerous."

SHADOWS OF DOMINION CITY

Max tightened his grip on his phone. "I have to be there, Sarah. This could be our only chance to find out who the Architect is—and to finally uncover what happened to Emily."

"Be careful, Max," she whispered. "I've seen what these people can do. You're risking everything."

As Max hung up, he took a last, lingering look around Wexler's hidden office. He knew he was walking into the lion's den, but there was no turning back. Wexler's death had unlocked new clues, but it also confirmed the severity of the threat he was up against. The Sovereigns' ritual of loyalty renewal, the Day of Reckoning, was about to unfold—and if he wasn't careful, he could be the next casualty.

Determined, he slipped out of the mansion and into the fading light, his path clear. The Dominion Club awaited, and with it, the truth that had evaded him for so long.

Max returned to police headquarters late in the evening, his mind racing with the new leads he'd uncovered in Wexler's mansion. As he reached his office, he noticed a flurry of activity down the hall near the holding cells. Officers were crowded around a figure being escorted into the precinct; his face partially obscured by the collar of his trench coat. Max's pulse quickened as he recognized the man: Martin Collins, an old friend of Senator Lawson and a prominent government official.

Max hadn't expected Collins to appear in this case. Collins had always presented himself as a family man, a public servant who kept his hands clean amid the political dirt of Dominion City. But Max had seen enough in his years on the force to know that appearances could be deceiving. If Collins was involved with The Sovereigns, it would be a revelation that could shake the case to its core.

He approached the crowd of officers just as Adrian stepped into the corridor, his expression smug and triumphant.

"Looks like we've got our man, Carter," Adrian announced, a slight sneer playing on his lips. "Collins was arrested based on an anonymous tip. He was meeting with Wexler the night of the murder."

Max narrowed his eyes. "An anonymous tip? And we're supposed to believe that?"

Adrian shrugged, feigning nonchalance. "The evidence speaks for itself. Collins's fingerprints were found at Wexler's mansion, and we've got surveillance footage placing him near the property around the estimated time of death."

Max's skepticism deepened as he watched Collins being led to the interrogation room. Something about this felt too convenient. An anonymous tip, perfect timing, and suddenly, a high-ranking official with connections to Lawson and The Sovereigns was brought in as a suspect. It was almost as if someone had gift-wrapped this lead for them.

"Let me talk to him," Max said, already heading toward the interrogation room.

Adrian's expression turned wary. "You think he's just going to confess to being part of some grand conspiracy? You're reading too much into this, Carter. Sometimes a suspect is just a suspect."

Ignoring Adrian's jab, Max entered the interrogation room, closing the door behind him. Collins sat at the table, his eyes darting around the room. He looked shaken, but he was attempting to hold onto a façade of composure.

"Detective Carter," Collins said, forcing a weak smile. "I didn't expect to see you here. I'm not sure what this is all about."

Max took a seat across from him, his gaze steady. "Mr. Collins, you were seen at Harold Wexler's property the night he was murdered. Surveillance footage places you near his home, and we have an anonymous tip suggesting you're connected to his death."

Collins's face fell, his confident mask cracking. "Detective, I can explain. I did meet with Wexler that evening, but it wasn't about anything... sinister."

"Then why the secrecy?" Max asked, crossing his arms. "You were close with Wexler. And as a friend of Senator Lawson, you're in a powerful position in the city. What were you meeting about?"

Collins hesitated, his gaze shifting as though searching for a way out. "It was a personal matter. Wexler... he was worried about some things he'd gotten involved with. He thought he could control them, but he was in over his head."

Max leaned forward, his voice low and firm. "You're talking about The Sovereigns, aren't you?"

Collins's face paled, and he looked away, his silence confirming Max's suspicions. Finally, he muttered, "Wexler was terrified. He said he'd seen things, things that made him question his loyalty. He wanted out, but we both knew that wasn't an option."

Max felt a surge of frustration. He knew Collins was holding back, afraid to reveal the full extent of his knowledge. "If you were trying to help him, why not go to the police? Why all the secrecy?"

Collins shook his head, his voice trembling. "You don't understand, Detective. The Sovereigns... they have people everywhere. People who can make things disappear, make people disappear. If Wexler tried to leave, he'd be dead. And now he is."

Max pressed on; sensing Collins was close to a breakthrough. "So why are you here, Collins? Why now?"

Collins looked up, desperation in his eyes. "I didn't kill him, Detective. I swear. Yes, I was there that night, but I left before... before anything happened. I got a call the next day saying that Wexler was dead, and I knew then that I was next."

Max felt a flicker of sympathy, but he kept his tone firm. "Then why not come forward? Why wait until you were dragged in?"

Collins sighed, running a hand over his face. "I was warned, Detective. Told to keep my mouth shut and keep my head down. They said if I made trouble, I'd be 'dealt with.' And then, just this morning, I found a note on my desk—a message telling me to go to Wexler's, to keep up appearances. That's when I knew... I was being set up."

Max's stomach twisted. He'd suspected a setup, but Collins's story only deepened his unease. Someone within The Sovereigns was orchestrating events to shift the blame, muddy the investigation, and throw him and Adrian off course. The cult was playing them, and Collins was just another pawn.

At that moment, Adrian entered the room, his face unreadable as he glanced between Max and Collins. "Carter, a word outside?"

Max rose, casting one last glance at Collins. "This isn't over, Collins. You might not have killed Wexler, but you know more than you're letting on."

Collins didn't respond, his face drawn with fear and resignation. As Max stepped into the hallway, Adrian closed the door behind him.

"What's the story?" Adrian asked, crossing his arms. "Did he confess?"

Max shook his head, frustration evident in his expression. "He claims he's being framed. Says he was set up by someone in The Sovereigns to throw us off."

Adrian rolled his eyes, exasperated. "Of course he'd say that. You're so focused on this cult theory that now every suspect is part of a 'setup.' You ever think he's just playing you?"

Max's patience snapped. "You're not seeing the bigger picture, Adrian. Collins isn't the mastermind here. Someone within The Sovereigns is manipulating us, controlling every step of this investigation. Wexler's murder, the message in blood—it's all part of their game."

Adrian's face twisted with irritation, but Max could see a flicker of doubt in his eyes. "All right, Carter. If you're so convinced, then prove it. What's your next move?"

Max took a steadying breath, organizing his thoughts. "We dig deeper into the message left at Wexler's house— 'Betrayed from within.' If there's a power struggle within The Sovereigns, then we need to identify who stands to gain from this. I want to know who sent that anonymous tip about Collins, and I want eyes on anyone close to Senator Lawson."

Adrian raised an eyebrow, still skeptical but intrigued. "So, you're saying someone in The Sovereigns is trying to throw us off and eliminate threats from within? You think Collins is just a scapegoat?"

"Exactly," Max replied, his tone intense. "The Sovereigns aren't just a group—they're a network, a hierarchy. Someone near the top is consolidating power, and they're using this investigation to cover their tracks. We need to look at the cult's leadership, starting with Lawson and anyone connected to him."

Adrian exhaled, his expression shifting to one of reluctant acceptance. "Fine. I'll dig into the tip. But if we're chasing phantoms again, this is on you, Carter."

Max nodded, feeling a renewed sense of purpose. Collins's arrest had been a distraction, a clever misdirection, but he now understood the deeper game. The Sovereigns had planted seeds of doubt to keep the police occupied while they purged their own ranks, ensuring their power remained intact.

As Adrian walked away, Max's thoughts raced with possibilities. He needed to get to the Dominion Club tonight, find any trace of The Sovereigns' power struggle, and expose the cult's true intentions. If Wexler's murder and Collins's arrest were just the beginning, then the stakes were higher than ever.

The Sovereigns were purging their own, preparing for a new chapter in Dominion City's history. And as long as Max stayed on their trail, he knew he was walking into the crosshairs of a ruthless enemy.

Chapter 6: Descent into Darkness

The city was blanketed in a thick, misty darkness by the time Sarah Blane arrived at Max's office. She was jittery, clutching a manila folder tightly in her hands, her face pale and eyes darting around as if she feared someone had followed her. Max noticed her anxiety the moment she stepped into the room, and he quickly closed the door, giving her a reassuring nod.

"Sarah, you're safe here," he said, his voice calm but encouraging. "What did you find?"

Sarah took a deep breath, forcing herself to sit down, and placed the folder on the desk between them. She looked Max in the eyes, her gaze determined but haunted. "Max, I wasn't sure if I should bring this to you. I didn't even know if I'd be able to decode it all... but it's Emily's. She left it behind, and I think she wanted someone to understand what she was uncovering."

Max leaned forward; his interest piqued as Sarah opened the folder. Inside were pages covered in handwritten notes and columns of symbols and numbers. Some were scrawled hastily, others more deliberate, as if Emily had been piecing together a puzzle that felt increasingly urgent with each discovery. Alongside the notes, Max saw newspaper clippings, photographs, and maps of Dominion City, all meticulously marked up in Emily's handwriting.

"I found these in her apartment," Sarah continued, her voice barely above a whisper. "It's a coded series of letters Emily wrote... They reveal The Sovereigns' structure, their hierarchy, and—most importantly—their plan for Dominion City. Max, she was documenting everything, every piece of evidence she could gather about this cult."

Max's pulse quickened as he sifted through the papers, his eyes catching on key phrases Emily had underlined in red ink. He began reading aloud, his voice tinged with disbelief. "The Architect... the Prophet... the Keeper... These are titles, roles within the cult."

Sarah nodded, her fingers nervously twisting together. "Yes. Each role has a specific function in maintaining their hold over the city. The Architect is the leader—the mastermind behind their operations, controlling the group's most secret plans. The Prophet is responsible for spreading the cult's influence through key figures, particularly in government and law enforcement. And the Keeper... they protect the cult's archives, a record of everyone who has been involved, their secrets, and the network of loyalty that binds them together."

Max's mind raced as he processed the information. This wasn't just a group of wealthy elites dabbling in secret societies for power—The Sovereigns were a calculated network, with each member serving a purpose. The level of organization was chilling, and it explained how they had operated in Dominion City undetected for so long. He glanced at Sarah, the weight of the discovery pressing down on him.

"If Emily was investigating their hierarchy," he said, "then she was onto something far bigger than any of us realized. This isn't just a political scheme—it's a coordinated effort to control Dominion City at every level. The Architect, the Prophet, the Keeper... they're positioning themselves to dictate the future of this city."

Sarah took a shaky breath, her fingers brushing over a particularly worn letter in the stack. "And there's more, Max. Look at this." She pulled out a sheet, handing it to him. The letter was filled with cryptic phrases, phrases like *"The Great Renewal," "The Blood Oath,"* and *"Sacrifice secures loyalty."* Emily had underlined these terms repeatedly, adding question marks in the margins as if even she hadn't fully grasped the significance.

Max's face darkened as he read, his mind whirling. "The Great Renewal... The Blood Oath... It sounds like some sort of ritual or ceremony. Maybe even a way to test loyalty within the cult."

Sarah nodded; her expression grim. "Exactly. Emily had circled this passage here—it says, *'The Renewal is both a rebirth and a reckoning. Loyalty must be absolute, or the Architect will cleanse us all.'* She was convinced this Renewal was tied to a ritual that would enforce loyalty and eliminate anyone who doubted The Sovereigns' methods."

Max felt a chill run down his spine. The Sovereigns' "Renewal" wasn't just a symbolic event—it was a purge, a means of weeding out dissent and solidifying control. It explained the recent murders, Wexler's brutal death, and the growing tension within the cult. He knew now that Emily's disappearance was likely tied to this ritual; she had known too much, and she had become a liability.

Max turned to another letter in the stack, this one marked with locations around the city: City Hall, The Dominion Club, Senator Lawson's Office. Each location was marked with a date and time, suggesting recent or upcoming gatherings.

"These are meeting spots," Max muttered. "They're coordinating their actions in real-time. The Sovereigns aren't just a shadowy force—they're actively moving, working together to ensure their plan for the city is airtight."

Sarah leaned forward, her voice barely a whisper. "There's one more piece, Max. One that's even more disturbing." She reached into her bag and pulled out a photograph. It was faded and grainy, as if it had been taken with a hidden camera. It showed a small group of people seated around a large, oval table in a darkened room, each person's face cast in shadows. At the head of the table sat a figure with an imposing presence, though his features were obscured. In the corner of the photo, someone had written a single word: *Architect*.

Max's breath caught as he examined the image. This was it—the Architect, the cult's elusive leader. Emily had managed to get this photograph somehow, but it had likely cost her dearly.

"Emily was close," Max murmured, his voice heavy with a mix of admiration and dread. "She'd found the Architect, or at least come close enough to get this photo. This is why she disappeared. They knew she was a threat."

Sarah looked down; her eyes filled with guilt. "Max, I should have helped her sooner. I thought she was over her head, chasing shadows. I didn't realize..."

Max placed a hand on her shoulder, his voice firm but gentle. "You're helping her now, Sarah. This information could save her life—and it could bring down The Sovereigns."

Just then, Max's phone buzzed with a notification. He glanced at the screen, and his stomach dropped as he read the message: "Another murder—Raymond Nash, the journalist. Same symbols, same method."

Max closed his eyes, the weight of the case pressing down harder than ever. Raymond Nash had been investigating Senator Lawson's connections to corruption. Now he was dead, killed in a way that mirrored Wexler's murder, with symbols left as another grim signature from The Sovereigns.

"Sarah," he said, his voice tight, "they're moving faster than we thought. This isn't just about Emily anymore. Anyone who tries to expose them—anyone who even comes close—is a target."

Sarah looked at him, her face pale but resolute. "What are you going to do?"

Max straightened, his resolve hardening. "I'm going to the Nash crime scene. I need to see if there's a connection between his investigation and what Emily uncovered. The Sovereigns are cleaning house, and we're running out of time."

Sarah nodded, her determination matching his. "Then I'll keep looking through Emily's notes, see if there's anything we missed. We need every piece of information if we're going to take them down."

Max gave her a grateful nod, slipping the photo of the Architect into his coat pocket. As he left his office, he felt the weight of the case press down on him, but he also felt a flicker of hope. With Sarah's help, he was closer to finding Emily—and to finally unmasking the Architect.

But as he headed toward the elevator, he couldn't shake the feeling that time was slipping away, and that the Architect was already one step ahead.

The next morning, police headquarters buzzed with tension, officers moving briskly through the halls as news of Raymond Nash's murder spread like wildfire. Max arrived early, still digesting the revelations from Sarah the night before. He'd barely had time to process the coded letters and chilling photograph she'd uncovered before another murder, another warning from The Sovereigns, added to the weight of the case.

He made his way toward the briefing room, where he knew Adrian would be waiting. But as he approached, he could already hear Adrian's raised voice through the half-closed door.

"Look, we have a prime suspect in Martin Collins," Adrian was saying, his tone laced with frustration. "He was seen at Wexler's house, his fingerprints were there, and he's tied to Lawson. I don't understand why we're still spinning our wheels on this Sovereigns nonsense."

Max clenched his jaw, pushing open the door. Adrian looked up, his eyes narrowing as he saw Max. Other officers turned, sensing the tension that had been brewing between the two detectives over the past few days. The rivalry between them had always simmered beneath the surface, but now, with a string of murders and The Sovereigns tightening their grip on Dominion City, it had reached a boiling point.

Max strode forward, his gaze unwavering. "Adrian, Collins is a red herring, and you know it. He's being used as a scapegoat to keep us off the real trail. The Sovereigns are behind these murders, and the evidence is pointing straight to their inner circle."

Adrian crossed his arms, his expression defiant. "The only evidence we have is a series of conspiracy theories and shadowy figures that might as well be urban legends. You're grasping at straws, Carter. Meanwhile, we have a concrete lead in Collins. I'm following it."

Max forced himself to stay calm, though the frustration gnawed at him. "Collins didn't kill Wexler, and you're wasting time trying to make him fit the narrative. Raymond Nash was murdered last night. He was an investigative journalist, and he'd been digging into Lawson's connections for months. The Sovereigns are eliminating anyone who could expose them, and you're playing right into their hands by going after a man they're framing."

Adrian rolled his eyes, his face twisting into a smirk. "Oh, I see. So now I'm the one who's falling for a trap? How convenient for you, Carter. You want to keep all the glory for yourself, keep Sarah's little discoveries to yourself, and act like you're the only one who can solve this case."

Max's fists clenched, but he kept his voice steady. "This isn't about glory, Adrian. This is about finding Emily Lawson, exposing The Sovereigns, and stopping these murders. Collins is a distraction. You know it, but you're so fixated on beating me that you're willing to ignore the truth."

Adrian's eyes narrowed; his jaw tight as he leaned forward. "You think you're the only one who wants to solve this case? I've been working just as hard as you, but you've been hogging all the leads, keeping Sarah's intel to yourself. I've had to do my own digging, follow my own leads because you won't share anything."

Max stared at Adrian, taken aback by the bitterness in his rival's voice. He hadn't realized how deep Adrian's resentment ran, how determined he was to prove himself—even if it meant taking dangerous shortcuts.

"Adrian," Max said quietly, trying to calm the tension. "This case is bigger than either of us. We're dealing with a cult that has a stranglehold on the city's power structure. If we don't work together—"

"Save it," Adrian snapped, cutting him off. "I don't need your help. I'm going to bring this case in myself, with or without your so-called leads. In fact, I've already got my own lead—a tip about an upcoming meeting with some of Lawson's associates. Maybe I'll get lucky and find the real killer."

Max's eyes narrowed. "A tip? From who?"

Adrian shrugged, feigning indifference. "Anonymous source. Said they had information on the murders and might be willing to talk. And unlike you, I'm not going to sit around waiting for another clue to drop into my lap."

Max felt a sinking feeling in his stomach. Adrian's desperation to solve the case on his own was making him reckless, and an anonymous tip could easily be another trap set by The Sovereigns. But before he could warn Adrian, his rival turned on his heel, his smirk returning.

"See you around, Carter," Adrian said, his voice mocking. "Maybe you'll get to follow in my footsteps for a change."

With that, Adrian strode out of the briefing room, leaving Max standing alone, a knot of worry forming in his chest. Adrian's ambition, his desire to prove himself, was driving him straight into the arms of The Sovereigns. Max could only hope his rival would realize the danger before it was too late.

Later That Day

Max tried to focus on his own investigation, but Adrian's departure weighed heavily on him. He couldn't shake the feeling that Adrian was in over his head, chasing a lead that was designed to lure him into a trap. Still, Max had no choice but to keep working, hoping he'd find something tangible before Adrian did something that couldn't be undone.

A few hours later, a message came through Max's phone. It was from Sarah, marked "Urgent." He opened it and found a link to an article she'd written that was just published, along with a brief note: *"Raymond Nash's final investigation. You need to read this."*

Max clicked the link, skimming the article. Sarah had written a powerful exposé on Nash's last investigation, detailing how he'd uncovered evidence that linked Senator Lawson to a secret network of influence and corruption. Nash had been working on exposing a covert group with connections reaching deep into the city's government and business sectors. Though he hadn't named The Sovereigns, the descriptions in the article pointed unmistakably to them.

Max's phone buzzed again, and this time it was a text from Sarah: *"Nash's last source was Adrian. He'd been feeding him leads for months. They were both getting close."*

Max felt a jolt of realization. Adrian's rivalry hadn't just been about proving himself—it was fueled by information Nash had been feeding him, likely hoping that a police ally could protect him. But now Nash was dead, and Adrian was diving into Nash's leads, determined to finish what the journalist had started.

His thoughts were interrupted as he got another text, this one from an officer on Adrian's team: *"Adrian is heading to the meeting point his source gave him. He didn't say where exactly, but it's somewhere near the Dominion Club."*

Max's chest tightened. He had to act fast. Adrian was walking into a trap, one likely orchestrated by The Sovereigns themselves. Without a moment's hesitation, Max grabbed his coat, racing out of the precinct and down to his car. He knew he was running out of time.

Dominion City Streets, Near the Dominion Club

Max parked a few blocks away from the club, keeping to the shadows as he made his way through the winding back alleys surrounding the upscale venue. The air was thick with the impending threat, and every sound seemed magnified as he drew closer. The Dominion Club loomed ahead, its grand entrance glittering under the streetlights, but Max knew Adrian wouldn't be approaching from the front.

He made his way around the side of the building, his footsteps light, his eyes scanning the darkness for any sign of his rival. Suddenly, he heard muffled voices echoing from an alleyway just beyond the club. He approached cautiously, peering around the corner, and froze.

Adrian was there, his face illuminated by the faint glow of a streetlamp as he confronted a group of men dressed in dark coats, their expressions hidden in shadow. At the center of the group stood a tall figure with a commanding presence, his voice smooth and low as he spoke to Adrian.

"Detective Cross," the man said, his voice cold and mocking. "So eager to find the truth. But you must understand... the truth is far more dangerous than you realize."

Adrian looked defiant, but there was a flicker of uncertainty in his eyes. "I know who you are. I know what you've done. You can't hide behind your secrets forever."

The man chuckled softly. "Oh, but secrets are what keep this city running, Detective. And those who pry too deep are rarely heard from again."

Max's pulse raced as he realized the danger Adrian was in. He was outnumbered, alone, and clearly underestimating the men around him. Just as Max was about to step forward, one of the men lunged at Adrian, grabbing his arm in a viselike grip.

Adrian struggled, but the others closed in, surrounding him. In a flash, Max made his decision. He stepped out of the shadows, his voice cutting through the tense silence.

"Let him go," Max demanded, his tone firm and unyielding.

The group turned, surprise flickering across their faces as they realized they weren't alone. Adrian's eyes widened as he saw Max, relief and frustration mingling on his face.

"Carter..." Adrian muttered; his voice strained.

The tall man, the one who seemed to be in charge, smirked, his gaze cold and calculating. "Another detective. How charming. But I'm afraid this conversation was private."

Max didn't flinch. "We know who you are, and we know what you're planning. You think you can silence everyone, but we're not backing down."

The man's smirk faded, replaced by a hard, menacing stare. "Then you should know, Detective Carter, that the consequences of your defiance will be... severe."

With a subtle gesture, he motioned to his men, who released Adrian. Max pulled Adrian back, and together they backed away, both aware that they'd narrowly escaped with their lives. The Sovereigns had issued their warning, and the message was clear: any further interference would be met with deadly force.

As they hurried down the alley, Max turned to Adrian, his voice low and urgent. "That was close. You need to stop running off like this, Adrian. This isn't a game."

Adrian's face was pale, his usual bravado shattered. He gave a small nod, shaken but resolute. "You're right, Carter. This isn't a game. But it's time we end it."

Max nodded, feeling a newfound sense of unity between them. They had both stared down The Sovereigns and survived, but now they had no choice but to bring the cult down—together.

The morning air was crisp and cold as Max arrived at the scene of yet another grim discovery. The building was an older apartment complex in Dominion City's downtown district, a place that had once housed prominent families but was now largely inhabited by writers, artists, and a few remaining die-hard locals. Police tape stretched across the entrance, blocking curious onlookers from the scene inside.

As Max ducked under the tape and stepped into the lobby, he was met by an officer who led him upstairs to the fifth floor. The hallway was quiet, with only the low murmur of detectives discussing the case as he walked. They stopped in front of a door that had been forced open, leading into the small apartment of Raymond Nash, the renowned investigative journalist known for exposing high-profile corruption. Nash had been relentless, and the articles he'd published had a specific focus: Dominion City's most powerful figures, including Senator Lawson.

Inside the apartment, the air was stale, tinged with a faint metallic scent that made Max's stomach tighten. Forensic techs worked carefully, gathering evidence from the scattered papers and books strewn across the small living room. Max took in the scene, noting the overturned coffee table, the broken lamp, and the bloodstains that streaked across the floor—a chaotic portrait of Nash's final moments.

At the center of it all lay Raymond Nash, sprawled on the ground near his desk. His face was pale, his eyes open and staring, as though frozen in defiance. Max felt a chill run down his spine. This wasn't just another murder; it was a message.

One of the forensics team members looked up, nodding in acknowledgment. "Detective Carter, it's as brutal as it looks. From the struggle, we'd guess he put up a fight."

Max stepped closer, his eyes drawn to a symbol scrawled hastily on the wall near Nash's body, written in blood. It was the three interlocking circles of The Sovereigns—the same symbol he'd seen at Wexler's murder. But this time, there was an additional detail: a single word written beneath it, smeared and barely legible. It read: *"Architect."*

Max felt the weight of the word sink in. The Sovereigns were making a point, marking their territory and leaving a breadcrumb trail that both taunted him and warned him to stay away. But if Nash had known the Architect's identity, if he'd been close to uncovering the cult's leader, then his death was more than just a silencing—it was a calculated elimination.

As he examined the scene further, Max noticed Nash's desk, covered in notes, newspapers, and what appeared to be a notebook filled with scrawled, hurried handwriting. His fingers brushed over the pages, noting keywords like *"Lawson," "Sovereigns,"* and *"The Great Renewal."* Nash had been on the same path as Emily, piecing together the cult's influence and preparing to expose them. But The Sovereigns had reached him first.

Just as Max was about to inspect Nash's notebook, Adrian appeared in the doorway, his face grim. He nodded curtly, stepping into the apartment with an uncharacteristic seriousness.

"Carter," he said, his voice low, "we need to talk."

Max looked up, catching the glint of unease in Adrian's eyes. For once, Adrian's usual cockiness had vanished, replaced by a look of genuine concern. He gestured to the hallway, and Max reluctantly followed, glancing back at the notebook before stepping out.

In the hallway, Adrian leaned against the wall, folding his arms. "I got a call this morning from someone claiming to be connected to The Sovereigns. They gave me a name—a source who might have ties to the Architect."

Max's eyebrows shot up. "You think it's legit? Or are they trying to lure you back in?"

Adrian shook his head, his gaze distant. "I don't know. But after last night... I can't ignore it. They want to meet tonight, and they're insisting I come alone."

Max's stomach clenched. It was dangerous, likely a trap. But if there was a chance of getting a name—of finally identifying the Architect—then it was a lead they couldn't afford to ignore.

"Then I'm coming with you," Max said firmly. "If they're setting you up, we need a backup plan."

Adrian hesitated, but finally nodded, his face tight with determination. "Fine. But we do this my way. I need to know that if it goes south, you'll stick to the plan."

Max gave a curt nod, sensing the severity of the moment. The rivalry between them was fading, replaced by a shared sense of purpose. They were both hunting the same enemy, both aware that they were closing in on something deadly.

As the forensics team continued their work, Max returned to Nash's apartment, drawn back to the notebook that had been left on the desk. He carefully flipped through the pages, skimming for anything that could give him an edge in the investigation. Halfway through, he found a section marked with red ink, where Nash had scrawled what appeared to be notes from a recent conversation.

"The Architect has a list. Targets. Purges of those who doubt."

"Lawson's involvement deeper than public record. Not just complicit—key figure."

"The Great Renewal approaches. Last chance to act before they consolidate power."

Max felt his pulse quicken. The Architect had a list of targets—people who knew too much, who threatened The

Sovereigns' plans. The recent murders were part of a larger pattern, a systematic purge of anyone who could expose the cult. And Senator Lawson wasn't just a passive player in this scheme—he was a central figure, perhaps even the Architect himself.

Max took photos of the notebook pages, documenting every detail before carefully setting it aside. Nash's work had been meticulous, and in his final days, he'd come dangerously close to the truth. But he had paid the ultimate price for his tenacity.

As he closed the notebook, Max noticed something else—an envelope tucked between the pages, sealed with red wax stamped with a single letter: *A*. Carefully, he broke the seal and unfolded the letter inside.

"To those who seek the truth, beware the path you tread. Dominion's fate is in the hands of those who keep their oaths. The Renewal is upon us, and the Architect's vision will shape the city anew. Any who resist will face the cleansing fire."

The message was cryptic, but it confirmed Max's fears: The Sovereigns were on the cusp of a major operation, one they believed would reshape Dominion City according to their vision. And anyone who stood in their way would be "cleansed."

Max felt a surge of urgency. Time was running out, and The Sovereigns' plans were accelerating. Nash's death, Wexler's murder, Emily's disappearance—it was all converging toward a single, terrifying conclusion.

He carefully pocketed the letter, knowing it could be the key to understanding the Architect's motives. As he left the apartment, he glanced back at Nash's desk one last time, a silent acknowledgment of the man's bravery. Nash had risked everything to expose the truth, and Max knew he couldn't let his death be in vain.

He had a new lead, a meeting to prepare for, and a city to protect. And this time, he was ready for whatever The Sovereigns had planned.

As night fell, a thick fog crept over Dominion City, wrapping the streets in an eerie silence. The glow from streetlights cast long shadows along the narrow alleys that wound their way through the city's center. Max and Adrian moved carefully through the darkness; their footsteps muffled as they neared the Dominion Club. The tip Adrian had received pointed to a secret gathering of Sovereign members at a nearby abandoned warehouse—a location that felt like a trap, but was too significant to ignore.

They stopped at the edge of a building, peering around the corner to where a narrow alley led to the back entrance of the warehouse. Dim lights illuminated the door, and two figures dressed in dark coats lingered outside, their stances guarded and alert.

Max looked over at Adrian, his voice barely a whisper. "Are you sure this is the place?"

Adrian nodded; his jaw set with determination. "This is where the tip said they'd be. The message was clear—they wanted me to come alone."

Max's expression darkened. "And yet, here I am. You really think they'll trust you enough to get you close to the Architect?"

Adrian shrugged, his eyes flashing with resolve. "I didn't come here to play nice, Carter. I came here for answers."

They took a moment to survey the entrance, noting the two guards who blocked the doorway. Max checked his watch; it was nearly midnight, the hour when the cult's gatherings were rumored to begin. This was the closest they'd come to the heart of The Sovereigns' operations, and both of them knew it.

"Here's the plan," Max whispered. "I'll create a diversion to pull the guards away. You slip inside and find a way to get close to the Architect. Just be careful—they're expecting someone tonight, and they won't hesitate to retaliate if they sense trouble."

Adrian gave a grim nod, his face etched with a seriousness Max had rarely seen. "I understand the risks. I'll be fine."

Max nodded, feeling a pang of concern but knowing there was no turning back. With a deep breath, he slipped around the side of the building, picking up a loose rock and tossing it against a metal dumpster nearby. The sharp clatter echoed through the alley, and one of the guards turned, gesturing for his partner to check it out.

As the guard approached, Max pressed himself against the wall, watching as the man stepped around the corner. In one swift motion, Max grabbed him, knocking him out with a precise hit. The second guard, distracted by the noise, had turned his back, giving Adrian the opportunity he needed. He slipped into the warehouse, disappearing into the shadows.

The warehouse interior was dimly lit, the air heavy with the scent of dust and decay. Adrian moved quietly through the maze of crates and abandoned equipment; his steps cautious as he followed the faint sound of murmured voices. He knew he was venturing deep into the cult's domain, but the prospect of getting close to the Architect kept him moving.

As he rounded a corner, he caught sight of a gathering in a large open space near the center of the warehouse. About a dozen figures stood in a circle, their faces hidden in shadow, their voices low and reverent. At the head of the circle was a tall, imposing figure dressed in a dark coat; his face obscured by a hood. Adrian's heart raced as he realized he was staring at the Architect.

The Architect's voice filled the room, smooth and authoritative, commanding the attention of everyone present. "Tonight, we reaffirm our commitment to Dominion City. The Great Renewal is upon us. Loyalty must be absolute."

The circle of figures responded in unison, their voices a whispered chorus. "Absolute."

Adrian's pulse quickened. This was it—the Architect, the figure who had orchestrated every move of The Sovereigns, was standing mere feet away, speaking openly of their plans. Adrian knew he had to get closer, hear more, find something that could finally bring the cult to light.

But as he edged forward, he stepped on a loose piece of debris that cracked beneath his foot. The sound was faint, but it was enough. The Architect paused mid-sentence, his head turning slightly toward the shadows where Adrian stood.

"Who's there?" the Architect demanded, his voice calm but laced with menace.

Adrian froze, cursing himself for the slip-up. For a brief moment, he considered retreating, but he knew this was his only chance. He straightened, stepping forward out of the shadows.

"It's me," he said, forcing a confidence into his voice that he didn't entirely feel. "I came to find the truth about The Sovereigns."

The Architect's face was still obscured, but Adrian sensed a smirk beneath the hood. The figures in the circle remained silent, their gazes fixed on Adrian, a mixture of surprise and amusement in their eyes.

"You must be Detective Cross," the Architect said, his tone both mocking and curious. "I was wondering when you'd make your appearance."

Adrian took another step forward, his eyes narrowing. "You've been running this city from the shadows, killing anyone who dares stand against you. But your time is up. People know. We know."

The Architect laughed softly, the sound echoing through the warehouse. "You think you're the first to make threats against me, Detective? Dominion City is full of people who believed they could change the course of power. But in the end, they either joined us or... vanished."

The crowd murmured in agreement, a low hum of approval that chilled Adrian to the bone. He forced himself to stand tall, his hands clenched at his sides.

"Where's Emily Lawson?" Adrian demanded, his voice steady. "What did you do to her?"

The Architect tilted his head, the shadows concealing his expression. "Emily was... misguided. She had the potential to join our cause, but she chose defiance. A pity. Defiance, as you'll soon learn, has a steep price."

Adrian's blood ran cold, his mind racing with the implication of the Architect's words. Emily had been close—too close to their secrets. And now, he realized, he was dangerously close too.

Suddenly, one of the hooded figures stepped forward, drawing a gun and pointing it at Adrian. "Enough talk. We warned you to stay away, Detective. You've ignored every warning."

The Architect raised a hand, stopping the gunman. "Wait. Let him go."

The others murmured in confusion, but the Architect's authority held them in check. He took a slow step forward, his gaze fixed on Adrian, his voice dropping to a low, menacing tone.

"I want you to understand, Detective," the Architect said softly. "I am giving you one final chance. Leave this case, forget what you've seen, and disappear from our affairs. Because if you continue, if you take one more step down this path, you will find that we are everywhere."

Adrian met the Architect's gaze, refusing to show fear. "I'm not backing down. I'll bring you down if it's the last thing I do."

The Architect's lips curved into a smile, a chilling expression of calculated control. "Then you'll share the same fate as the others who thought they could resist."

The Architect gestured to the guards, who reluctantly lowered their guns. Adrian felt a surge of both relief and dread. He had been spared, but only as a pawn in the Architect's twisted game. The Sovereigns were toying with him, daring him to continue, knowing that any further defiance would mean his end.

The figures closed in around the Architect, turning back to their ritual as Adrian slowly backed away, his mind racing with the implications of the encounter. He had glimpsed the Architect's power, felt the weight of the cult's reach. And as he exited the warehouse, he knew that every step from here on was a step into deeper darkness.

Adrian slipped out of the building, and they disappeared into the night, but the Architect's warning echoed in his mind, a dark promise that Dominion City was already theirs—and that any resistance would be crushed.

Chapter 7: Finding the Cult

The dim light of the early morning seeped through the windows of police headquarters, casting long shadows across Max's cluttered desk. He sat hunched over, rifling through a pile of notes, maps, and hastily scribbled timelines, every detail a clue in his desperate search to find Emily Lawson. Beside him, Adrian Cross leaned back in his chair, his jaw clenched as he scanned Sarah's most recent update. The weight of urgency was thick in the room, a suffocating presence that neither man could ignore.

Sarah had sent a flurry of texts just before dawn, each more urgent than the last. She had uncovered evidence suggesting that Emily's disappearance wasn't just a case of revenge or silencing dissent—it was part of something much larger, something both terrifying and ritualistic. Max's pulse quickened as he read the messages again, his mind piecing together Sarah's findings like jagged puzzle pieces.

Sarah's texts had been explicit: *"The Sovereigns plan to sacrifice Emily at the upcoming summit. It's their way of solidifying power, their 'offering' to their cause. They'll use the summit as cover. You have less than 48 hours to stop it."*

Max looked up at Adrian, his face grim. "We don't have much time. If Sarah's information is right, The Sovereigns are planning to use Emily's death as a public display of their power. This ritual isn't just a show of loyalty—it's a message to anyone who might oppose them."

Adrian nodded, his expression a mixture of determination and frustration. "And they've covered their tracks well. We've spent weeks chasing leads that went nowhere, all while they prepared for this. If we don't stop them now, Emily's life won't be the only thing they take—they'll tighten their grip on Dominion City."

They poured over Sarah's notes, which laid out the cult's timeline for the summit. According to Emily's research, the Sovereigns' hierarchy had planned this event for years, waiting for the perfect moment to reinforce their influence. The summit was set to be a landmark occasion for Dominion City's elite, a gathering of politicians, powerful business leaders, and government officials—all figures under the Sovereigns' control.

Max tapped a map of the city, highlighting locations that the cult used as regular meeting spots. "These are places where Emily tracked them before her disappearance. We'll have to focus on the most likely locations they'd use for a ritual. Somewhere isolated but symbolic—a place they can control, but close enough to the summit to keep their cover."

Adrian studied the map, his brow furrowing as he analyzed the spots. "They'll want a location that's meaningful, that reinforces their message. Somewhere grand, but hidden."

Max nodded, his gaze settling on a spot that had come up frequently in Emily's notes: St. Michael's Chapel. It was an abandoned cathedral on the edge of Dominion City, once a place of worship but now a crumbling relic known for its eerie beauty. It had been repurposed by the city council as an event space, but it remained mostly unused—a forgotten landmark, shrouded in darkness.

"This could be it," Max murmured, tracing his finger along the map to St. Michael's. "It fits. They'd have privacy, enough room to host the ritual, and it's close enough to the city center that they could blend in with summit attendees. Emily noted several suspicious activities near the chapel last month, but she wasn't sure if they were connected."

Adrian nodded; his eyes sharp with focus. "Then we start there. If they're holding Emily, she's running out of time. And if we're wrong…" He trailed off, the unspoken consequence lingering heavily between them.

Max leaned back, his mind racing through the possibilities. He knew this might be their only chance, and that failure meant not only losing Emily but cementing the Sovereigns' control over Dominion City. He had felt the pressure before, but this time, it was different. It was personal.

Adrian looked over, sensing Max's tension. "We're getting close, Carter. But we can't afford any more missteps. We'll need a plan if we're going to get in there, find Emily, and get her out alive."

Max met Adrian's gaze; their rivalry momentarily set aside by the urgency of their mission. "Agreed. We can't go in without knowing what we're up against. Sarah's intel says they'll have guards, cult members stationed outside to keep intruders out. If we're going to infiltrate, we'll need to blend in."

Adrian frowned, considering the logistics. "The Sovereigns use masks for their inner ceremonies, right? And robes—it's part of their way of keeping everyone anonymous and loyal. We could use that to our advantage. If we can get our hands on their disguises, we might be able to move through the crowd unnoticed."

Max nodded, feeling a flicker of hope. "We can get close enough to survey the place first, see how many members they've stationed outside. We'll go in under cover, find where they're holding Emily, and get her out before the ritual begins."

Adrian straightened; his expression resolved. "And if we have to fight our way out?"

Max gave a grim smile. "Then we'll make sure we take down as many of them as we can. But we'll need to be strategic. If this goes wrong, Emily isn't the only one who won't make it out."

The gravity of their plan settled over them, each of them feeling the weight of what lay ahead. Max's thoughts drifted to Sarah, the risks she'd taken to uncover the cult's secrets and bring them closer to the truth. She'd sacrificed her own safety to help them, and now, they were racing against time to make sure her work wasn't in vain.

Max turned his gaze back to the map, his finger still hovering over St. Michael's Chapel and Brookes Worth mansion. "We need to gather whatever we can—flashlights, radios, anything that might give us an edge. And we need to make sure Sarah has someone watching her. If we're close, they might come after her next."

Adrian gave a curt nod. "I'll make the calls, arrange for protection. But we need to move fast. If we don't show up by tomorrow morning, this city will wake up to a Sovereign-run council."

The two men stood in silence, a shared understanding passing between them. They were about to enter enemy territory, infiltrating the heart of a deadly cult that held nothing but contempt for those who defied them. And they both knew that only one thing mattered now: saving Emily and stopping the ritual before the Sovereigns' power was solidified forever.

Max took a steadying breath, feeling the weight of the mission settle over him. "Let's get ready. This is our one shot to take them down, and if we do this right, it'll be the end of the line for The Sovereigns."

Adrian nodded, a flicker of determination in his eyes. "We'll bring them down, Carter. We'll make sure they never hold this city in fear again."

With that, they set off, each man steeling himself for the task ahead. As the first light of dawn broke over Dominion City, they knew it might be the last dawn they'd see. But the Sovereigns had left them no choice; they would confront the cult in their ritual chamber, fight to save Emily, and bring the entire network crashing down.

And this time, there would be no turning back.

Max and Adrian maneuvered through the dim corridors of the abandoned Brookes Worth Mansion, their flashlights slicing through the heavy darkness. This sprawling, decaying estate on the outskirts of Dominion City had been one of the locations Sarah had flagged as a potential Sovereign hideout, and the hurried messages they'd intercepted earlier that day suggested that the cult was actively using the place.

"Stay close," Max whispered as they stepped into a grand, dust-covered foyer. Fractured moonlight spilled through broken windows, illuminating the peeling wallpaper and once-grand chandeliers, now draped in cobwebs. The atmosphere was oppressive, the mansion exuding a haunted stillness that made Max's skin crawl. He knew they were running out of time, but every instinct warned him to tread carefully.

Adrian scanned the shadows, his flashlight sweeping over antique furniture cloaked in dust and sheets. "Hard to believe this was once one of the grandest homes in Dominion. Now it's just a tomb."

Max's jaw clenched. "The Sovereigns seem to have a thing for forgotten places. Out of sight, out of mind. Let's hope they haven't taken Emily somewhere even more remote."

They moved through the foyer, the silence broken only by the creak of old floorboards under their feet. The house's layout was vast and maze-like, each turn revealing endless hallways, branching staircases, and rooms filled with relics of a time long gone. It was the perfect place for someone to hide—or to be hidden.

Max pushed open a set of double doors leading into a spacious parlor. His flashlight caught a glint of something metallic on the floor—a bracelet. He crouched down, recognizing it as a charm bracelet. Emily's.

"This was hers," he murmured, holding up the delicate piece of jewelry. "She was here, Adrian. We're on the right track."

Adrian examined the bracelet, his expression darkening. "If she was here, then they're moving her fast. They're trying to keep us guessing."

They searched the room, finding a few more belongings scattered across the floor—a torn scrap of fabric, a notebook with hastily scrawled notes. Max flipped through the pages, his heart racing as he read Emily's handwriting. The pages were filled with observations about the cult's members and rituals, clues she must have gathered while investigating them on her own. But the last entry, scrawled hastily and barely legible, made his blood run cold: *"The Renewal is upon us. They have chosen me."*

Adrian's gaze met Max's; his face set with grim determination. "They're getting ready to move her. They want to make her the centerpiece of this ritual."

Max shoved the notebook into his pocket. "Then we're close. She left these behind for us to find. She's trying to lead us to her."

They continued their search, moving deeper into the mansion. Each room felt like a dead end, empty and echoing, the tension mounting with every corner they turned. After what felt like hours of searching, they reached the mansion's basement, a series of twisting, narrow corridors carved into the stone foundation. The air was colder here, thick with the scent of damp earth and mildew. Max's flashlight flickered, casting strange shadows along the rough stone walls.

"This has to be it," Max muttered, stepping cautiously into the basement's depths. "They'd want a place that's secluded, away from prying eyes."

Adrian gripped his flashlight tightly, his eyes scanning each shadow. "Let's hope so. Because if this isn't it—"

He was cut off by a distant sound, a faint scuffling echoing down the corridor. Max held up a hand, signaling for silence, and they both stilled, listening intently. The sound grew louder, the unmistakable shuffle of footsteps approaching from the far end of the basement. Max motioned for Adrian to take cover behind a stack of old crates as he pressed himself against the wall, peering around the corner.

A figure emerged, dressed in the dark robes and mask of a Sovereigns member. The man seemed to be searching the basement, his movements deliberate and purposeful. Max felt a surge of adrenaline as he realized they were finally face-to-face with one of the cult members.

Adrian tensed, his eyes meeting Max's with a nod of understanding. They waited, holding their breath as the figure passed by, oblivious to their presence. Just as he neared the exit, Max lunged forward, grabbing him from behind and covering his mouth. The man struggled, but Adrian quickly moved in, helping Max subdue him without a sound.

"Where's Emily Lawson?" Max demanded, keeping his voice low and urgent. "Where is the ritual taking place?"

The man's eyes widened, but he stayed silent, his gaze defiant. Adrian pressed the edge of his flashlight against the man's throat, a warning in his expression. "You'd better talk. We know what's going on, and we're not leaving without answers."

The cult member finally broke, his voice low and strained. "She's... she's here. But you're too late. The ceremony will begin, and The Sovereigns will have their Renewal."

Max exchanged a look with Adrian, his instincts screaming that this man was lying. But before he could press further, the man's gaze shifted, a sinister glint appearing in his eyes.

"They're expecting you," he whispered, a slight smirk twisting his lips. "We knew you'd come."

Realization dawned on Max, and he felt a cold dread settle over him. They had been led here deliberately, drawn to the mansion to be kept busy while the real ritual took place elsewhere. His grip on the man's collar tightened, fury sparking in his eyes.

"Where's the actual ritual?" Max demanded, his voice like steel. "Where are they holding Emily?"

The man's smirk deepened; his expression maddeningly calm. "You'll never find it. The Architect has planned for everything. By the time you figure it out, the Renewal will be complete."

Max clenched his jaw, knowing he was wasting time. They needed a new plan, and fast. Leaving the cult member tied up in the basement, he turned to Adrian, his face etched with determination.

"We're back to square one," Max muttered. "This place was a diversion, meant to keep us here while they prepare for the ritual somewhere else. They're always one step ahead."

Adrian nodded; his own frustration evident. "Then we need to move faster. If they wanted us here, then it means the real location is close. We have to think like them—find somewhere that's symbolic, hidden, but powerful enough to host a ritual of this scale."

Max's mind raced as he sifted through what they knew about the Sovereigns. They had a penchant for places rich with history, buildings that had long been associated with power or mystique. And then, like a flash, it came to him.

"St. Michael's Chapel," he said, his voice sharp with certainty. "We considered it earlier, but it felt too obvious. But they knew we'd think that."

Adrian's eyes narrowed in understanding. "They wanted us to dismiss it, to rule it out because it was too visible. But it's perfect—a place with history, secluded, and big enough to host their ceremony."

Without another word, they turned and hurried out of the mansion, racing against time as they headed toward St. Michael's. The Sovereigns had tried to throw them off, to lead them down false trails and waste precious time. But now, Max and Adrian knew they were close. Emily was somewhere in that chapel, and the ritual was about to begin.

As they drove through the darkened streets, the city lights flashing by in a blur, Max felt a renewed sense of purpose. He had been deceived, tricked into following empty trails and chasing false leads. But this time, he wouldn't stop until Emily was safe, and The Sovereigns' hold on Dominion City was shattered.

He clenched his fists, the determination in his voice unwavering. "They're not getting away this time. Whatever it takes, we're ending this."

Max and Adrian moved through the shadows of St. Michael's Chapel, blending in with a steady stream of masked figures entering the building. The chapel's heavy wooden doors creaked shut behind them, sealing out the world beyond. Inside, the air was thick with a sense of dread, the silence broken only by the faint echoes of footsteps on the stone floor.

The chapel's interior was vast, illuminated by candlelight that flickered from alcoves lining the walls. Gothic arches loomed above them, casting dark shadows across the pews, which were arranged in orderly rows facing the altar. The whole space felt charged with anticipation, as if the very walls knew a sinister event was about to unfold.

Max scanned the room, looking for any sign of Emily or the cult gathering Sarah had described. But to his frustration, the main hall was nearly empty, save for a few robed figures who milled about in silence, setting up what looked like ceremonial candles and incense burners around the altar.

"This doesn't make sense," Max murmured under his breath, his voice muffled by the mask. "Where's everyone else?"

Adrian's eyes narrowed as he scanned the area. "Maybe we missed something. They wouldn't hold a major ritual out in the open like this. There's got to be another space, somewhere hidden."

They split up, moving cautiously through the empty aisles and checking each alcove, feeling along the walls for any hidden doors or passages. The chapel was a labyrinth of corridors and back rooms, each one colder and more silent than the last. Every turn they took only seemed to deepen the oppressive atmosphere, but they found nothing to suggest a gathering was underway.

Frustration gnawed at Max as he reached the far end of the chapel, his patience running thin. Just as he was about to turn back, he noticed a faint scraping sound echoing from beneath his feet. He knelt down, pressing his ear to the floor, straining to make out the muffled voices drifting up from below.

"They're below us," he whispered urgently to Adrian, who had joined him.

Adrian's eyes widened, his voice a tense whisper. "There must be a basement or catacombs beneath the chapel. Let's look for a way down."

They continued searching, their fingers brushing over cold stone and wood, feeling for any slight give. Near the altar, Max's hand finally caught the edge of a trap door, barely visible against the stone floor, its seams disguised as part of the chapel's intricate tilework. He exchanged a look with Adrian, nodding in silent agreement.

Max gripped the metal ring embedded in the trap door and slowly lifted it, revealing a set of stone steps that descended into darkness. The air that wafted up was stale and cold, carrying a faint, metallic scent that made his stomach twist.

"Ready?" Adrian asked, his voice barely above a whisper, his gaze steady but tense.

Max nodded; his jaw clenched. "Let's go."

They descended the narrow staircase, the darkness thickening as they moved deeper beneath the chapel. The walls were close and damp, the rough stone brushing against their robes as they carefully navigated the steps. Their flashlights cast weak beams that barely cut through the dark, illuminating only a few feet ahead. At the bottom of the staircase, the passage opened into a long, narrow hallway lined with worn, ancient tapestries and dimly flickering torches.

Voices echoed faintly from the end of the corridor, a low hum of chanting that sent a chill down Max's spine. He could make out words here and there, twisted phrases invoking power, loyalty, and sacrifice. It was The Sovereigns' ritual, unfolding just ahead.

"They've already started," Adrian whispered, his voice tense. "If Emily's part of this ritual, we're running out of time."

Max nodded, his pulse pounding in his ears. They followed the corridor to a pair of heavy wooden doors that marked the entrance to the ritual chamber. The chanting grew louder, reverberating through the stone walls. Max and Adrian took a deep breath, steeling themselves, and slipped through the doors.

In the basement, surrounded by relics of forgotten gatherings, Max and Adrian continued their search with growing urgency. The room was dense with the remnants of past church events—dusty hymnals, rusted chairs, a pile of old tablecloths that had yellowed over time. The faint smell of mildew mixed with an odd metallic tang in the air, and a weighty silence hung around them, broken only by the scuff of their footsteps.

Adrian moved aside a stack of hymn books and was greeted by a tattered piece of paper pinned to the wall. He tugged it down, squinting at the crude map that unfolded in his hands. "Max, look at this."

Max stepped closer, his eyes scanning the paper. Faded lines traced the outline of the town's waterfront, marked with an 'X' at the docks.

His jaw tightened. "The docks... this is where they were planning on performing the ritual. This chapel must have a passage leading to the docks."

Max's face darkened. "They must've been using this church basement as a hideout—or at least a meeting point. Maybe it's where they kept Emily before they moved her."

Max clenched his fists, the realization hitting him hard. "The Sovereigns must've moved her because they knew we were coming. They're always one step ahead."

Adrian's hands tightened around the map, his jaw set. "Then we'll have to catch up."

Together, they followed the map through the hidden passageway to the docks, stepping out into the cold night with newfound resolve. The docks awaited them, and whatever they'd find there—answers, danger, or even a trap—would be met head-on.

Chapter 8: The Rescue Attempt

Max and Adrian crouched in the shadows outside an unmarked warehouse next to the docks, their breaths shallow as they scanned the area. The building loomed ahead, its walls thick with grime and rust, but behind its unassuming exterior lay the cult's innermost sanctuary, the heart of The Sovereigns' cult. This was the culmination of their investigation—the place where everything, including Emily's life, hung in the balance.

"Ready?" Max whispered, his eyes meeting Adrian's in the darkness.

Adrian gave a curt nod, his expression a mixture of determination and dread. "Let's end this."

They moved quietly toward the back entrance, slipping past two guards who were busy inspecting their surroundings. Max held his breath as they reached the door, silently grateful for the cover of night. Once inside, they stepped into a huge room that seemed to pulse with an eerie red glow. Symbols and sigils were drawn on the walls, the paint dark and ominous against the steel. The air was thick with the smell of incense and something metallic—blood, perhaps.

Max and Adrian moved with purpose, pressing themselves against the wall as they approached a doorway. The muffled sounds of chanting echoed from deeper inside, a chilling rhythm that reverberated through the walls. Max's pulse quickened as he realized they were getting closer to the ceremony, but the path ahead was far from clear.

Max paused, peering inside. The room was arranged like a twisted temple, with rows of benches facing a central altar draped in dark cloth. Massive, wrought-iron chandeliers hung from the ceiling, casting an unsettling glow over the cultists who filled the room. Each of them was cloaked in dark robes, their faces hidden behind grotesque masks adorned with symbols of power and allegiance.

And at the center of it all was Emily.

She was bound to the altar, her wrists and ankles secured with iron shackles, her face pale and expression weary but defiant. Max felt a surge of relief and fury. They'd found her, but the Sovereigns had positioned her as the centerpiece of their twisted ceremony.

Adrian noticed her as well, his eyes narrowing as he took in the scene. "We need a way to get close without drawing attention," he whispered.

Max nodded, his mind racing. They couldn't simply storm the room—there were too many cultists, and the Architect would surely have guards stationed at every exit. He pointed to the far end of the room. If they could find another way around, they might be able to get closer to the altar without attracting attention.

Moving cautiously, they slipped outside, keeping to the building as they searched for an alternate entrance. The chanting grew louder, the words becoming clearer, as if each syllable held a sinister power. Max's stomach twisted as he caught snippets of the ceremony, phrases invoking "dominion over the city" and "renewal through sacrifice."

They reached a side door and slipped through it, entering what looked like a preparation chamber. Ritual tools and candles cluttered a long wooden table, and on the far wall hung a large tapestry depicting the Sovereigns' symbol—the three interlocking circles, embroidered in crimson and gold. Adrian's jaw clenched as he took in the opulent display.

"Twisted, isn't it?" he muttered, barely containing his disgust. "They see themselves as some kind of nobility, chosen to 'lead' the city through fear and control."

Max nodded, his gaze lingering on the tapestry. "And they think Emily's life is just a piece in their game. We're not letting this ritual finish."

Max's breath caught as he studied the Architect. The leader's movements were calm, deliberate, and authoritative, every gesture exuding control. The Architect's mask was intricately detailed, unlike the others—its surface gleamed in the candlelight, etched with symbols that seemed to shift and shimmer. As he watched, the Architect raised his arms, signaling the cultists to begin the final part of the ritual.

"Tonight, we embrace the Renewal," the Architect intoned, his voice echoing through the hall. "Through sacrifice, we reaffirm our dominion over Dominion City. This offering will bind us, strengthen us, and ensure our future."

The cultists responded in unison, their voices blending into a low, sinister hum. Max felt a chill run down his spine. They were running out of time—if they didn't act soon, Emily would become another victim, her life extinguished to satisfy the Sovereigns' delusional vision of power.

"We make our move now," Max whispered, turning to Adrian. "We create a distraction, pull their attention away from Emily. If we can cause enough confusion, we might have a chance to reach her."

Adrian nodded; his expression grim but determined. "I'll circle around to the opposite side and create a diversion. Once I've got their attention, you go for Emily."

Max gripped his shoulder briefly, meeting his gaze. "Be careful, Adrian. They're ruthless, and they won't hesitate to kill."

Adrian gave a tight nod, then slipped away into the shadows, moving toward the far side of the room. Max watched him go, his mind already racing with his next steps. He'd need to be quick, precise, and ready for anything.

Moments later, a loud crash echoed from the opposite end of the room as Adrian kicked over a table, sending ritual candles scattering across the floor. The sudden noise startled the cultists, and several of them turned, their attention drawn to the commotion. Adrian made sure to keep their focus, knocking over another table and shouting a taunt that echoed through the room.

"Is this your idea of power?" he yelled, his voice defiant. "Hiding behind masks and rituals? You're nothing but cowards."

The Architect's head snapped toward the noise, his posture stiffening. He gestured to a group of guards, who quickly moved toward Adrian, their weapons drawn. But the distraction worked—most of the cultists' attention shifted toward Adrian, leaving Max with a narrow but vital opening.

Taking a steadying breath, Max slipped through the crates until he reached the edge of the altar. Emily's eyes widened as she saw him approach, a glimmer of hope sparking in her gaze.

"Max..." she whispered, her voice hoarse. "I thought—"

"No time," he whispered back, reaching for the chains binding her wrists. "We're getting you out of here."

As he worked to free her, Emily's gaze darted around the room. "The Architect... he's more powerful than we thought. They all follow him like he's some kind of dark prophet."

Max didn't look up, his focus on the chains. "I know. But not invincible. He'll fall just like the rest of them."

Just as he loosened the final chain, a shadow fell over them. Max looked up, his heart pounding as he met the cold, unfeeling gaze of the Architect, who stood towering above them, flanked by two guards.

The Architect's voice was calm, almost amused. "Did you really think you could disrupt the Renewal, Detective Carter? The Sovereigns are eternal. You are nothing but a brief inconvenience."

Max rose to his feet, positioning himself between Emily and the Architect. "You're done, Architect. Dominion City won't be yours to manipulate anymore."

The Architect tilted his head, a mocking smile hidden beneath his mask. "Such noble words. But you fail to understand—Dominion City already belongs to us. And nothing you do can change that."

At a signal from the Architect, the two guards lunged forward. Max braced himself, meeting them head-on in a brutal clash. He fought with everything he had, his movements fueled by desperation and anger. Emily scrambled back, pressing herself against the altar as the cultists swarmed, their chants growing louder, their fanaticism undeterred.

Across the room, Adrian fought off a group of cultists, his defiance as fierce as Max's. The Architect watched them both, his gaze cold and calculating. He held up his hand, and the chanting ceased, the room falling silent as the cultists turned their attention back to him.

"Tonight, you witness the power of the Sovereigns," he intoned. "And tonight, you will see that nothing can stop us."

With a wave of his hand, more guards closed in on Max and Adrian, surrounding them as the Architect stepped back, watching with calm satisfaction.

Max and Adrian exchanged a look, each of them bruised and exhausted but resolute. They knew the odds, knew they were outnumbered and cornered. But they also knew that this was their one chance to break the cult's hold on the city. And for that, they were willing to risk everything.

Together, they braced themselves for the final fight, each of them determined to save Emily and end the Architect's twisted vision for Dominion City—no matter the cost.

The make shift sanctuary of the Sovereigns' cult throbbed with tense silence as Max and Adrian stood side-by-side, encircled by dark-cloaked figures who stared at them with chilling calm. The Architect loomed above them on the dais, his mask glinting in the dim light, his bearing imperious and unyielding. Emily was just behind him, her face a mixture of defiance and terror. Max's heart pounded as he gauged the odds, his mind racing as he formulated a plan. They were surrounded, outnumbered, and trapped, but he couldn't afford to let fear control him. Emily's life depended on them staying strong.

The Architect's voice broke the silence, his words a low, dangerous murmur that carried across the room. "Detectives Carter and Cross... How predictable that you would end up here, at the feet of the Sovereigns, struggling to protect a city you cannot control."

Max clenched his fists, his voice steady. "Your control ends tonight, Architect. We're taking Emily, and we're ending this sick empire you've built."

The Architect chuckled softly, the sound echoing ominously. "Is that so? You are nothing but pawns in a game that was decided long before you were even aware of it. I knew you'd come—I've been counting on it."

Adrian's jaw tightened, his eyes narrowing. "Then why haven't you stopped us? If you're so powerful, why are we still standing here?"

The Architect tilted his head, studying Adrian with a gleam of amusement. "Because, Detective Cross, you're exactly where I want you. You have been from the beginning." He paused, letting his words sink in. "I needed a dogged, ambitious investigator—someone to draw attention away from the deeper workings of the Sovereigns. And you fulfilled that role perfectly."

Adrian's face twisted in confusion and anger. "What are you talking about?"

The Architect took a measured step forward, his gaze locked onto Adrian. "You, Detective Cross, were chosen for this case. Do you really believe you just happened to fall into our path? From the moment you started pursuing the Sovereigns, you were on a leash—our leash. Your so-called investigation has been nothing more than a clever ruse to keep you and your department busy while we expanded our reach, unchecked."

Max felt a chill creep down his spine as he saw the impact of the words on Adrian's face. Adrian's expression shifted from defiance to disbelief, and finally to devastation. He had been used, manipulated by the very cult he'd fought so hard to expose. Every step he'd taken, every lead he'd pursued—it had all been part of the Architect's master plan.

Adrian's voice shook as he spoke, a mixture of betrayal and fury coloring his words. "You... you set me up. Made me chase shadows while you pulled the strings. You used me."

The Architect's smile widened behind his mask. "Precisely. Your ambition, your rivalry with Detective Carter... it was all so easy to stoke. You played your part beautifully."

Max could see the turmoil raging within Adrian, his anger and sense of betrayal threatening to tear him apart. But they didn't have time for Adrian to process it. Emily was still in danger, and the Sovereigns wouldn't hesitate to carry out the ritual.

"Adrian," Max said, his voice urgent but calm. "They might have used you, but you're here now. We're in this together. Let's end this."

Adrian's eyes flicked to Max, a spark of determination rekindling. He nodded, his jaw set as he pushed aside the weight of his anger and betrayal. They'd deal with the fallout later—right now, they had a job to do.

The Architect raised his hand, signaling to his followers. "End them," he commanded coldly, his voice reverberating through the room.

At his signal, the cultists closed in, their movements synchronized, their faces hidden behind emotionless masks. Max and Adrian braced themselves as the first wave descended upon them, fists and weapons raised. The fight was brutal, each strike driven by sheer survival instinct. Max ducked under a swinging blade, countering with a well-aimed punch that sent his attacker sprawling to the floor. Adrian fought with raw intensity, his anger fueling each hit, each block, each kick as he defended his position.

The cultists were relentless, their attacks swift and calculated. Max's muscles burned as he parried blow after blow, his vision narrowing as he focused on reaching Emily. He caught her eye across the room, her expression a mix of hope and terror, and it gave him the strength to keep fighting. He couldn't let her down.

The Architect watched from his elevated position; his calm demeanor unshaken by the chaos unfolding below him. He seemed almost amused by the struggle, as if it were all part of some grand performance crafted for his amusement.

"Do you see, Detective?" the Architect called out over the noise, his voice taunting. "Your resistance is futile. Dominion City belongs to us—our influence is woven into the very fabric of its power. You may kill a few, but the Sovereigns are eternal."

Max's fists clenched as he fought his way toward the Architect, rage simmering beneath his focus. "Not if we can help it," he snarled, elbowing another cultist out of his path. "Your influence dies with you."

Finally, they reached the dais, standing mere feet from the Architect. But before they could advance, the Architect held a blade against Emily's throat, his hand steady, his eyes cold.

"One more step," he warned, his voice a low, menacing growl. "And she becomes my final offering."

Max froze, his heart pounding as he calculated their options. Emily looked at him, her eyes wide with fear but also trust. She believed in him, even now.

"Let her go," Max said, his voice calm but fierce. "She has nothing to do with your sick plans. This is between us."

The Architect's gaze remained fixed on Max, his grip on the blade unyielding. "You misunderstand, Detective. She has everything to do with it. Through her sacrifice, we ensure our dominion, our renewal. Without it, our vision for Dominion City cannot proceed."

In that moment, Adrian made his move. With a swift, silent motion, he lunged forward, catching the Architect off-guard and knocking the blade from his hand. Emily staggered back, her hands free, as Max rushed to her side, pulling her away from the Architect's reach.

But the Architect recovered quickly, his gaze hardening as he signaled to the remaining cultists. "Kill them," he spat, his voice filled with a venomous intensity.

The cultists descended upon them in a final, desperate attempt to complete their leader's orders. Max and Adrian fought with everything they had, each move driven by the knowledge that failure was not an option. They took down cultist after cultist, their bodies moving in sync as they defended Emily and each other.

In the chaos, Max saw an opening. He grabbed the fallen blade, gripping it tightly as he moved toward the Architect. The cult leader, finally sensing that his control was slipping, backed away, his mask hiding any hint of fear. But Max could see it in his eyes—the realization that his empire was crumbling.

With a final, determined swing, slicing the Architect's robes. He staggered, his feet faltering as he fell back, hitting his head on a nearby anvil, his body fell limp as he slid down to the floor.

The room fell silent, the remaining cultists frozen as they watched their leader collapse. Without the Architect, the Sovereigns' cult was shattered, their control broken. Slowly, one by one, the cultists dropped their weapons, some removing their masks as the weight of their leader's downfall registered.

Max took a deep breath, his gaze lingering on the Architect's still form he walks over and removes the mask from the Architect seeing it was Marus Dalton. It was over. The Sovereigns' reign over Dominion City was finally over.

He turned to Adrian and Emily, his expression a mixture of relief and exhaustion. Adrian looked back at him, his face filled with the same disbelief, the same hard-won sense of victory. Emily, still shaken but safe, managed a faint smile, her eyes brimming with gratitude.

"Is it... is it really over?" Emily asked, her voice barely a whisper.

Max nodded; his own relief evident. "Yes. It's over."

Adrian placed a hand on his shoulder, a silent acknowledgment of the battle they had fought, the battle they had won. They had survived the Sovereigns, and now Dominion City could begin to heal.

As they made their way out of the warehouse, the first light of dawn began to break over the horizon, casting a faint glow over the city. They had brought down the cult that had haunted Dominion City for far too long, and in the light of the new day, they felt a sense of hope—a hope that, after everything, they had reclaimed their city from the darkness.

As the dawn light seeped through the broken windows of the cult's warehouse, Max, Adrian, and Emily moved cautiously toward the exit, their steps slow and tentative. They had won, but the weight of what they had just experienced hung heavily in the air, an ominous reminder that their battle against the Sovereigns wasn't over yet. Every sound seemed amplified in the sudden quiet of the docks, the silence after the fight thick and almost suffocating.

Emily leaned on Max, her strength waning as the adrenaline began to wear off. She was pale and exhausted, her clothes torn, but her spirit unbroken.

But just as they reached the waters front, a slow, mocking clap echoed from behind them. The sound was chilling, each clap deliberate, like a twisted metronome in the hollow building. Max's stomach clenched as he turned to see a figure emerging from the shadows—a tall man, cloaked in darkness, his face hidden beneath an elaborate, blood-red mask.

The figure's voice was low and smooth, dripping with contempt. "Impressive, detectives. Truly impressive. You managed to take down one man. But the Sovereigns... the Sovereigns are not so easily dismantled."

Max's heart sank. He recognized the voice immediately—it was one of the Sovereigns' most influential members, Councilman Douglas Reyland, a man who held significant sway in Dominion City's political circles and had publicly supported Senator Lawson for years. Reyland was known for his charisma, his charm, his carefully crafted public persona. But now his true nature was on full display.

"Reyland," Max muttered, his voice filled with a mix of disbelief and anger. "So, you're the real leader of the Sovereigns. Marcus was just your puppet."

Reyland tilted his head, the faintest hint of a smile visible beneath his mask. "Oh, the Architect served his purpose well. A figurehead to rally the faithful, to instill fear in those who dared oppose us. But the Sovereigns... we're much more than any one man. We're an idea, Detective Carter. And ideas, as you know, are indestructible."

Adrian's fists clenched, his expression darkening. "You think you can just walk away? That after everything you've done, you can hide behind that mask and disappear into the city?"

Reyland chuckled, "I don't need to disappear, Detective Cross. Dominion City is already mine. I hold the power, the influence, and the loyalty of men and women who will ensure that my work continues. Kill me, arrest me—do whatever you like. The Sovereigns will live on, long after this day."

Max took a step forward, his voice low and filled with defiance. "We'll see about that. We've exposed you, Reyland. We'll bring the truth to light. The people of Dominion City will know who you really are."

Reyland's smile widened; his confidence unwavering. "And who will believe you, Detective? Who will believe that a respected councilman, a figure of authority, is the leader of a secret cult? No... even if you reveal everything, I will always be one step ahead. I hold the evidence, the connections. And your precious city will remain under my control."

Max's mind raced, searching for any weakness, any leverage they could use. Reyland was right; even with the Architect dead and the ritual disrupted, the Sovereigns' influence reached further than they could grasp. The cult was rooted in the very fabric of Dominion City's power structure. Reyland didn't need a mask to operate—his real face held just as much power.

As if reading Max's thoughts, Reyland took a step back, his gaze steady. "Enjoy your little victory, detectives. You've earned it. But know this—while you celebrate, we will rebuild. Dominion City will always belong to us, and you will always be too late to stop us."

He turned to leave, his calm demeanor infuriatingly intact. But before he could take another step, Adrian lunged forward, his voice a low growl. "Not this time, Reyland."

Max held Adrian back, his grip firm. "He's right, Adrian. We can't touch him here. Not without hard evidence."

Adrian's eyes burned with fury; his frustration palpable. But he took a deep breath, backing down as Reyland disappeared into the shadows.

Once Reyland was gone, Emily looked up at Max, her voice trembling. "What... what now? If he's right, if the Sovereigns still have power—"

Max squeezed her shoulder, his gaze resolute. "Then we expose them. We gather every piece of evidence, every witness. We fight them in the light."

Adrian nodded, his jaw set. "And we start with Reyland. He may think he's untouchable, but he made a mistake tonight. He showed his face, and we'll use that against him."

Max took a deep breath, feeling the weight of the mission ahead. The fight against the Sovereigns wasn't over—it had only just begun. But now, with Emily safe and Reyland's true identity revealed, they had the upper hand, a crack in the cult's armor that they could exploit.

Together, leaving the darkness behind as the first rays of dawn broke over Dominion City. The night had been long and brutal, but they knew now what they were up against. And they would stop at nothing to bring down the Sovereigns once and for all.

But as they walked into the light, each of them felt the ominous shadow of Reyland's promise lingering—a warning that Dominion City's fight for freedom was ongoing.

Chapter 9: Exposing the Cult

The city was waking up, but the three of them felt like survivors emerging from a nightmare. Max kept a firm grip on Emily's arm, steadying her as they navigated the quiet streets. Adrian walked a few paces ahead, his gaze scanning their surroundings for any sign of cult members who might still be in pursuit.

Finally, they ducked into an alley, catching their breath in the brief silence that followed. Emily leaned against the wall, exhausted but safe, her eyes closed as she fought to steady her breathing. Max took a moment to examine her, searching her face for signs of lingering fear. But despite her ordeal, he saw a flicker of determination in her gaze.

"Thank you," she whispered, looking from Max to Adrian. "For not giving up on me. I didn't think... I didn't think I'd make it out."

Max placed a reassuring hand on her shoulder. "You were brave, Emily. Braver than anyone could have asked for. But it's not over yet."

Adrian cleared his throat, nodding toward the crumpled bag he'd grabbed before they left the warehouse. "I think we might have something that could end this for good." He opened the bag, revealing a stack of documents, some hastily bound together and marked with the Sovereigns' familiar symbol of three interlocking circles.

Max took the papers, sifting through them quickly. Even at a glance, he could tell they held critical evidence against the cult. Financial records, payments made to various officials, correspondence between high-ranking members—each piece painted a vivid picture of how deeply the Sovereigns' influence extended through the city's power structures.

Max held up a letter, his eyes scanning the lines of meticulously typed text. "They were paying off council members, police officers, judges. Everyone who mattered. The Sovereigns had a stranglehold on this city for years."

Adrian looked over his shoulder, his face grim. "And here's proof of donations to Senator Lawson's re-election campaign. They were backing his political rise, ensuring he'd protect their interests from the inside."

Emily's face tightened, her voice barely a whisper. "So that's why they took me. To control him. They needed to ensure his loyalty."

Max nodded, the pieces falling into place. "The Sovereigns' network wasn't just a cult—it was a power machine. They were willing to silence anyone who got in their way. And you... you were their leverage."

The sound of approaching footsteps made them all stiffen, and Max quickly tucked the documents back into the bag. He peeked around the corner, his heart racing, but relaxed slightly when he saw Sarah approaching, her face a mix of relief and concern as she caught sight of them.

"Thank god you're safe," she said, reaching out to Emily and pulling her into a tight hug. "We've been searching everywhere for you."

Emily clung to Sarah; her relief evident as she finally let herself breathe. "They were... they were going to kill me, Sarah. As part of some ritual. They said my death would 'renew' their power."

Sarah's face darkened; her voice barely controlled. "We'll make sure they never have that power again. Did you find anything? Anything we can use?"

Max held up the bag of documents, a glint of hope in his eyes. "We did. This is everything. It's a record of everyone they paid off, every alliance they forged. If we use this right, we can bring them down."

Adrian's expression hardened, a sense of purpose settling over him. "Then we don't waste any time. We get these documents to the chief, and we expose every last one of them."

Max's thoughts churned as they began to make their way toward police headquarters. They had tangible proof in their hands—evidence that could tear apart the Sovereigns' web of influence. But he knew it wouldn't be easy. The cult's roots ran deep, and there were still powerful figures within the city who would fight to protect their empire.

As they walked, Sarah pulled Max aside, her voice low. "You know they'll fight back. They have connections, resources. This won't be over until every last one of them is brought to justice."

Max's eyes narrowed, his jaw set. "I know. But we're not backing down. They've taken too much, hurt too many people. It's time to finish this."

When they arrived at headquarters, the tension was palpable. The chief met them in a small, private conference room, his expression a mix of disbelief and grim determination as Max laid the documents on the table. Emily, still visibly shaken, sat beside Sarah, who kept a protective arm around her. Adrian paced, his anger and frustration evident in his every movement.

The chief flipped through the papers, his face growing darker with each page. "This... this is explosive. We're talking about some of the city's most powerful people—judges, politicians, law enforcement officers. If this gets out, Dominion City will be turned upside down."

Max nodded, his voice steady. "It has to get out. The Sovereigns have controlled this city long enough. We can't let them keep hiding behind masks and money."

The chief looked at him, a flicker of admiration in his gaze. "You're right. But this won't be easy. People with this kind of power won't go down without a fight."

Adrian stopped pacing, his voice hard. "Then we prepare for that fight. We issue warrants, arrest those we can. And for the ones who evade us? We keep pressing. We make sure they know we're not stopping."

Max felt a surge of determination. They were finally on the brink of dismantling the cult that had haunted Dominion City for years, and he wasn't about to let anything stand in their way. He looked at Emily, her gaze filled with a quiet strength, and knew that their fight had taken on a new urgency—not just to bring justice to the city, but to protect everyone the Sovereigns had hurt.

The chief cleared his throat, glancing at the officers who had begun to gather around the table. "Then let's get to work. Every officer here is now part of this operation. We're going to take down the Sovereigns piece by piece. It won't be easy, and it won't be fast, but this is where we make our stand."

As the officers moved into action, Max felt a sense of purpose settle over him. The Sovereigns' influence was vast, their reach deep, but they were no longer untouchable. They had left behind the evidence, and now Dominion City was waking up to the truth.

Adrian joined him by the window, staring out over the city with a hardened expression. "This is it, Max. The beginning of the end for them."

Max nodded; his voice resolute. "And we won't stop until every last one of them is brought down."

Together, they watched as the city came alive, knowing that this was just the start of their battle. The Sovereigns' network might be unraveling, but Max and Adrian both understood that the cult's remaining members would do everything in their power to survive.

For now, though, they had the upper hand—and they weren't about to let it go.

The day was slipping into late afternoon by the time Max, Adrian, Sarah, and Emily gathered in the precinct's conference room, the fluorescent lights casting a harsh glare on the piles of evidence and documents they'd collected. Outside, Dominion City's streets pulsed with the usual bustle, its citizens unaware of the revelations that were about to shatter their perception of their leaders and institutions. Inside, tension filled the room as they prepared to launch the operation that would expose the Sovereigns.

Max glanced at the organized stacks in front of him—files of financial records, photos of secret meetings, letters, and emails detailing the Sovereigns' hidden hand in nearly every corner of the city's infrastructure. Sarah worked quickly at a laptop, uploading files to secure servers and making copies for the press, while Adrian paced near the doorway, his brow furrowed with a mix of anticipation and dread.

The chief entered; his face grim. "Are we ready to move on this?"

Max nodded, gesturing to the evidence. "This is everything we've managed to piece together. With this, we can expose the

Sovereigns' influence over the city's political and legal systems. This operation, the bribes, the connections—it's all here."

The chief's gaze swept over the documents, his eyes lingering on the names of well-known officials, respected council members, and prominent judges. "These people hold power over Dominion City's future. This is going to shake things up like nothing we've ever seen before."

Emily, seated beside Sarah, looked up, her voice steady despite the faint tremor of exhaustion. "They used me. They used my father. This has to come out. The people of Dominion City deserve to know the truth."

Adrian stepped forward, his voice hard. "We have warrants ready for immediate arrests. Some of the Sovereigns' key members are still within reach, but others have gone underground. Reyland and his allies will try to buy time, to regroup. We have to make our move before they disappear completely."

The chief nodded; his face set with determination. "Then we start with what we have. We'll issue warrants, coordinate with trusted officers, and arrest those we can. I'll make the call to City Hall—by tomorrow morning, Dominion City will know exactly who's been pulling the strings."

As the chief left to mobilize the officers, the room buzzed with urgency. Max, Adrian, Sarah, and Emily moved quickly, gathering more files, organizing more leads, and calling in backup. Every detail mattered, and they couldn't afford any mistakes.

An hour later, Through the windows, they could see squad cars pulling up to the courthouse, City Hall, and private residences. Officers emerged, some carrying warrants, others following orders to guard entrances and exits. News had already begun to leak, and whispers of the Sovereigns' influence over Dominion City's highest offices were spreading through the press like wildfire.

Emily watched the commotion outside, a quiet intensity in her gaze. "It's strange," she said, her voice thoughtful. "These were people my family trusted—people we thought were doing good for this city."

Sarah placed a hand on her shoulder, her own expression somber. "It's hard to believe how deep corruption can run. But today, we're doing something about it."

Suddenly, Adrian's phone buzzed, jolting him from his thoughts. He glanced at the screen, his jaw clenching as he read the message. "Reyland and several others are evading arrest," he muttered, his voice laced with frustration. "They must have been tipped off. Some of their assets were transferred out of the country just hours ago."

Max exchanged a glance with Adrian, both of them realizing the implications. "They've had contingency plans in place for years," Max said, the weight of the realization settling over him. "They knew this day might come, and they're not going down without a fight."

The chief re-entered the room, his face tight with anger. "Some of our key targets have gone into hiding. We've arrested half a dozen high-ranking members, but several of the Sovereigns' core leaders—including Reyland—have vanished."

Max's hand clenched into a fist, a simmering frustration building in his chest. "Reyland must have connections abroad, resources he can tap into if he needs to disappear. He won't make it easy for us to find him."

Adrian's eyes narrowed, his jaw set. "But we won't stop looking. This is just the beginning—we'll dismantle every last piece of their network, and we'll track him down no matter how long it takes."

Sarah stepped forward; her gaze fierce. "I'm going to make sure the press knows exactly what's happening. We may not have caught Reyland yet, but we have enough to expose the cult's influence over the city. By tomorrow, Dominion City will know that their leaders were complicit in a conspiracy."

The chief nodded; his expression resolute. "Then let's make it public. The lighter we shine on this, the harder it'll be for any of them to stay hidden."

Later that evening, As the news broke, Dominion City was thrown into a frenzy. Headlines blared across every news station and website: *"Secret Cult Controls Dominion City's Power Structure," "Councilman Reyland and Other Officials Implicated in Sovereign Conspiracy,"* and *"Evidence Reveals Deep-Seated Corruption."*

Sarah and Emily watched the coverage from a monitor in the precinct's conference room, their faces reflecting a mixture of relief and exhaustion. For Emily, it was a moment of validation—a public acknowledgment of the horrors she had endured. Sarah's expression was one of fierce satisfaction, knowing her reporting had finally brought to light the darkness that had plagued the city.

Meanwhile, Max and Adrian sat in silence, the gravity of their victory tempered by the knowledge that the battle wasn't over. As reporters interviewed city officials, legal experts, and witnesses, both detectives knew that many Sovereign members were still at large, hiding in the city's shadows.

"We did it," Max said finally, his voice low. "We exposed them."

Adrian nodded, though his face was dark with lingering doubt. "But we didn't get all of them. Reyland, Lawson, and who knows how many others—they're still out there. Free to regroup, to start over."

Max placed a hand on Adrian's shoulder, his voice steady. "They're weakened, Adrian. Their influence is crumbling, and the city knows who they are now. We'll keep hunting them down, one by one. This isn't over, but we're not fighting alone anymore."

Adrian nodded slowly, his resolve returning. But as he glanced back at the screen, he couldn't shake the feeling that this victory, as monumental as it was, came at a cost. His own ambition, his desire to prove himself, had been twisted by the very people he'd sought to bring down. And now, he was left with the bitter realization that he'd played into the cult's hands, a pawn in their grand scheme.

Max seemed to sense his thoughts; his voice quiet. "You couldn't have known, Adrian. None of us did."

Adrian's jaw clenched, his gaze hard. "I should have. I was too blinded by rivalry, too focused on proving myself. And they used that against me. But not anymore." He looked at Max, a new determination in his eyes. "From now on, we do this right. No shortcuts. We bring them down by the book."

Max nodded, a hint of pride in his gaze. "Agreed. They thought they could divide us, use us against each other. But they underestimated us."

Together, they turned back to the screen, watching as the news coverage continued to spread the story of the Sovereigns' downfall. The city was finally beginning to wake up to the truth, and though Reyland and his allies had slipped through their grasp, Max and Adrian knew that their work was far from finished.

As the night deepened, they felt a renewed sense of purpose. Dominion City's fight for justice was far from over, but they had taken the first step toward reclaiming it from the shadows. And this time, they wouldn't stop until every last remnant of the Sovereigns was wiped out.

Later that night, the precinct was nearly empty, its hallways lit by the dim glow of security lights. Max sat alone at his desk; his eyes fixed on a worn photo frame he held in his hands. The picture inside was faded, the colors softened by time, but he could still make out the familiar, comforting smile of his wife, Lauren, her arm draped around his shoulders on a bright summer day long ago.

He'd spent years haunted by the mystery of her death, every lead slipping through his fingers, every clue fading into silence. But tonight, as he stared at her photo, he felt a strange mixture of sorrow and closure settling over him. The Sovereigns had been involved in her case, their network of corruption protecting those who had orchestrated her murder to keep her silence. She'd been investigating city officials for years, collecting evidence of corruption, and had gotten too close to uncovering their secrets.

It had been the Sovereigns' way of handling threats: calculated, clean, and final. They'd silenced her to keep their empire intact, to protect their shadowy interests and twisted ideology. And all these years, Max had carried the burden of her loss, blaming himself for not being able to save her.

As he looked at the photo, he finally let himself mourn, not with the blinding anger he'd carried for so long, but with a quiet grief. She had always known the risks of pursuing the truth, and though he hadn't been able to protect her, he had fulfilled her legacy. He'd finished what she'd started, unraveling the web of corruption she'd died trying to expose.

A soft knock on his door broke him from his thoughts. Adrian stepped in, his face shadowed, his shoulders tense as he looked at Max. He held two cups of coffee, setting one on the edge of Max's desk before pulling up a chair.

They sat in silence for a moment, each lost in their own thoughts. Finally, Adrian spoke, his voice low and rough. "I've been doing a lot of thinking, Max. About everything—my role in all of this, the way I was used."

Max looked over, listening as Adrian struggled to find the right words.

"I was so focused on proving myself, on beating you," Adrian continued, his eyes downcast. "I didn't see how they were manipulating me, feeding my ambition to keep me chasing my own tail. Every case, every rivalry... it was all part of their plan to keep us divided."

Max took a deep breath, his voice steady but empathetic. "They were powerful, Adrian. They knew how to exploit people, especially people with a fire for justice. You wanted to do good, but they twisted that. None of us saw it coming."

Adrian let out a bitter laugh. "I was supposed to be the one with the edge, the one with all the answers. But in the end, I was just another pawn in their game. And I hate knowing that I played right into their hands."

Max placed a hand on his shoulder. "You weren't just a pawn, Adrian. You were a threat to them. You and I together? We're a lot harder to break. They knew that, and they tried to turn us against each other. But look at where we are now. We exposed them, together."

Adrian's expression softened, the weight of his regret momentarily easing. "Maybe you're right. But I still feel like I let the city down. Like I let myself down."

He looked out the window, his gaze distant. "It's strange. My whole career, I've chased every lead, every case, like it was a chance to prove myself. But now... I'm starting to realize it's not about winning. It's about getting justice, real justice."

Max nodded; his own voice filled with a quiet conviction. "Justice is messy, and it's rarely clean. But it's what we signed up for. And sometimes, it's the small victories that make all the difference."

Adrian met his gaze, a flicker of determination returning to his eyes. "From now on, I'm not going to let ambition cloud my vision. We do this right, Max. We go after every last one of them, by the book."

Max raised his coffee cup in a silent toast, a hint of a smile on his lips. "Together."

They clinked their cups, a symbolic gesture that cemented their alliance, their friendship. For the first time in years, there was no rivalry between them, only a shared mission—a commitment to restoring justice in a city that had long been ruled by shadows.

Meanwhile at Sarah's apartment, Sarah and Emily sat across from each other in Sarah's cozy living room, the remnants of hastily ordered takeout containers strewn across the coffee table. Emily had finally showered and changed, and while she still looked pale and worn, there was a spark of resilience in her eyes.

Emily looked down, her fingers fidgeting with her tea cup. "You think the arrests will stick? That this will really change things?"

Sarah's expression softened. "It won't be easy. People like Reyland don't go down without a fight. But we've taken the first step. We've shown the city what's been hiding in plain sight, and now they can't turn a blind eye."

Emily nodded, her voice wavering. "For so long, I thought they had everything under control—that there was nothing we could do to fight them. They're... they're so powerful."

Sarah reached across the table, taking Emily's hand. "That's how they operate—through fear and silence. But that's over now. We've shined a light on them, and now the whole city knows the truth. They may be powerful, but they're not invincible."

A look of determination settled over Emily's face. "I want to help, Sarah. I don't want to be a victim anymore. I want to make sure that no one else has to go through what I did."

Sarah smiled, a warm, proud expression. "Then let's keep fighting. The Sovereigns may be wounded, but they're not gone. We'll make sure that every last one of them faces justice."

Emily took a deep breath, her resolve strengthening. Together, they clinked their tea cups, a toast to resilience, to survival, and to the long road ahead.

Back at the Precinct, Max and Adrian watched the city lights from the window, each lost in thought, each feeling the weight of their choices, their actions, and the personal toll the case had taken. They were battered, scarred, but they had survived.

Adrian broke the silence, his voice quiet but resolute. "It feels like we're just getting started. There are still so many out there, hiding, waiting to take back control."

Max nodded; his expression serious. "And we'll be there every step of the way. They can hide, they can try to run, but they'll never take this city again."

As they stood in silence, a shared understanding passed between them. They had both lost something to the

Sovereigns—Max, his wife; Adrian, his sense of purpose—but in fighting together, they had found a new path forward, a commitment to the truth that would guide them in the battles yet to come.

And as the night deepened over Dominion City, the two detectives knew one thing with unshakable certainty: they had reclaimed their city from the shadows. And though the fight wasn't over, they would face it together, until every last remnant of the Sovereigns was brought to justice.

Chapter 10: Dominion's Downfall

Dominion City's downtown square was a sea of people. Crowds packed the streets in front of City Hall, holding up signs and shouting in anger and frustration. News vans lined the sidewalks, broadcasting the scene to every screen in the city, while reporters interviewed distraught citizens and local activists. The city, usually calm and composed, was now filled with an electric, tense energy—a storm brewing over the revelations of the Sovereigns' corruption that had shaken Dominion to its core.

Max stood at the edge of the crowd, watching as the people he'd spent his career protecting grappled with the truth. It was overwhelming to see. Hundreds of citizens, some of whom he recognized from his years on the force, held up signs that read, *"End the Corruption!"* and *"We Deserve Justice!"* Their voices echoed through the square, a chorus of rage and betrayal aimed at the very leaders they had once trusted.

"This city is ours, not theirs!" a man shouted, his voice filled with fury. "They've been lying to us for years!"

Max's phone buzzed in his pocket. It was Sarah, who was nearby, covering the protests for her paper. She waved him over to where she stood with a group of journalists, her expression a mixture of exhaustion and resolve.

"They're not holding back," she said, gesturing to the crowd as she joined him. "This is bigger than anything Dominion City has ever faced."

Max nodded, his eyes scanning the crowd. "They deserve to be angry. This city was their home, and the Sovereigns turned it into a playground for power and manipulation. The people were pawns in their game."

As the crowd continued to grow, Max spotted familiar faces on the large screen set up by the press. News stations were cycling through images of powerful leaders and officials who had been implicated in the Sovereigns' corruption network. The faces of Councilman Reyland, Senator Lawson, and other elite figures flashed across the screen, each accompanied by critical captions: *"Tied to the Cult," "Bribed by the Sovereigns," "Above the Law No More."*

The chief of police emerged from City Hall and stepped up to a hastily arranged podium. His face was grave, his eyes tired. The crowd quieted, tension thickening in the air as everyone waited to hear what he had to say.

"My fellow citizens," he began, his voice echoing across the square, "what has been uncovered in our city over the last few days is shocking, and, like many of you, I am heartbroken and enraged. The Sovereigns operated in the shadows, taking advantage of positions of power to control this city. I want you to know that I and everyone in this department are committed to bringing every last one of them to justice."

A murmur rippled through the crowd, some people nodding in agreement while others muttered in disbelief. Max felt the heavy reality of the moment settle over him—there would be no quick or easy fix. The Sovereigns' grip had spread too far, their influence too deep.

Suddenly, a young woman in the crowd shouted, "How can we trust you? You're part of the system! How do we know you're not one of them?"

The chief's face tightened, but he kept his composure. "I understand your distrust," he replied, his voice steady. "We know the damage that has been done, and we are taking every measure to ensure transparency and accountability. Many officers have already been suspended and are under investigation. From this moment on, Dominion City's police force will serve the public without exception or favor."

Beside him, Sarah nodded in quiet approval. "It's a start," she murmured to Max. "But it's going to take more than promises to rebuild this city."

As the chief continued, a young man held up a sign reading, *"Justice for the Victims!"* His voice trembled with emotion as he spoke to the reporter nearby. "My sister died because of the drugs the Sovereigns smuggled into our neighborhoods. She was just a kid. How do they think they can just walk away from this?"

Max's heart clenched. He knew this man's pain all too well—the Sovereigns had left countless scars on Dominion City, and justice, even if served, wouldn't heal all of them.

Nearby, Adrian stood with a small group of officers, watching the scene with a conflicted expression. He'd been used by the Sovereigns, a pawn in their scheme to protect their own. Now, seeing the fallout, he felt a weight settle over him, a responsibility to make things right. He stepped toward Max, his eyes filled with determination.

"This isn't going to be over for a long time," Adrian said, his voice low but resolute. "But we're not backing down. We're going to keep fighting, even if it takes years to root them all out."

Max gave a slight nod, a grim smile crossing his face. "One by one. They'll try to disappear, to wait this out. But we'll be here when they try to come back."

Just then, the crowd's attention turned to the screen, where a news anchor announced breaking developments. *"Several high-profile members of Dominion City's elite are already under arrest, including business magnates, judges, and city council members. However, Councilman Douglas Reyland remains at large, and sources suggest he may have fled the country."*

A collective murmur of anger rippled through the crowd, voices rising in frustration. "They let him go! He's escaping!" someone shouted. Others took up the cry, their anger spilling over.

Adrian clenched his jaw, feeling the frustration of those around him. "Reyland can't hide forever," he said. "We'll find him."

Max watched as the crowd's anger continued to build, but he knew that in their fury lay something more important—a city's collective refusal to be controlled. This was what the Sovereigns had tried so hard to suppress, and it was that spirit that gave him hope for the first time in years.

One voice rose above the others, a woman holding a sign that read *"Hope and Justice for All."* Her words carried through the crowd; her tone fierce. "This city is ours now. No more shadows, no more secrets. If they think they can hide, they're wrong. We'll be watching."

Max felt a surge of pride and purpose as he watched her words ripple through the crowd. The people of Dominion City weren't broken—they were angry, hurt, but ready to reclaim their city.

Sarah, standing beside him, leaned in and said, "It feels like the city's waking up."

Max nodded, his eyes never leaving the crowd. "And this time, they won't be fooled. We'll make sure of it."

As the rally continued, Max felt the weight of the past few days shift, replaced by a sense of resolve. Dominion City had been scarred, but its spirit was alive and strong. The Sovereigns had tried to control it, to crush its will, but they had failed. And now, with the city's support and its people demanding justice, he knew the sovereigns couldn't stay hidden for long.

The precinct was unusually quiet as Max, Adrian, Sarah, and Emily gathered in a dimly lit conference room, surrounded by stacks of files, maps, and computer screens glowing with surveillance images. The immediate threat of the Sovereigns had been exposed, but a new, more elusive enemy lingered in the form of those who had escaped the initial arrests. Councilman Douglas Reyland and other high-ranking Sovereign members remained unaccounted for, and the reality of their unfinished work weighed heavily on them all.

Sarah stood by a map pinned to the wall, where she'd marked locations rumored to have ties to the Sovereigns. Her hand traced over several pins clustered around the city's outskirts—safehouses, warehouses, and isolated estates that served as meeting points for members still at large.

"These are the places we haven't been able to search yet," Sarah said, her voice tense. "Our sources think that some of the Sovereigns' top members, including Reyland, may have used these as safehouses in the days leading up to the arrests."

Adrian leaned in; his gaze sharp as he studied the map. "If we can get a team to each of these sites, we might be able to catch them before they have a chance to regroup."

Max nodded, feeling a renewed sense of purpose. "The ones still out there won't wait for long. They know we're closing in, and they'll be doing everything they can to cover their tracks or relocate. We can't let that happen."

Emily, who had been quiet until now, spoke up, her voice filled with quiet determination. "There's more. Reyland and his inner circle didn't just have safehouses in Dominion City. They owned properties in nearby towns, other states. He talked about them in his notes, called them 'sanctuaries' for when things got too hot here."

Max and Adrian exchanged a look. If the Sovereigns had established sanctuaries outside Dominion City, then this was bigger than they'd initially thought. The network they'd been fighting wasn't just a local organization—it had connections beyond the city, perhaps even nationwide.

Max's mind raced. "If that's true, we'll need more resources than what we have here. We'll need to coordinate with other jurisdictions, get cooperation from federal agencies."

Adrian nodded; his voice laced with urgency. "We may be dealing with Sovereign cells spread across the region. If we can confirm their ties to Dominion City, we might finally have enough leverage to bring them down."

Sarah pulled out her laptop and brought up several emails and encrypted documents she'd uncovered while investigating. "I managed to decode some of Reyland's correspondence. He referred to key Sovereign leaders by code names— 'The Banker,' 'The Shadow,' and 'The Patriot.' These people aren't just followers; they're figureheads, each one in charge of different aspects of the organization. Reyland might have been the public face here, but there are others working in the shadows."

Emily leaned closer, pointing to a specific email exchange. "This message here—it mentions a vault. Reyland kept referring to it as 'The Legacy.' He said it contained 'the future of the Sovereigns' and that it was to be moved to a secure location in case of an emergency. Whatever 'The Legacy' is, they're treating it as something sacred."

Max felt a chill run down his spine. "A vault? If it's a place where they store records, artifacts, or funds, then it could contain everything we need to map out their operations. Financial records, member lists, blackmail material—they'd keep it all safe, under lock and key."

Adrian crossed his arms, his gaze intense. "But where would they hide something that valuable?"

Sarah clicked through a few more documents, her expression thoughtful. "According to these messages, the vault was never kept in the city itself. It's likely stored somewhere remote, possibly at one of those safehouses or even outside state borders. Reyland and his closest allies would have access to it—and if they've fled, it's possible they're headed straight for it."

Emily added, "Reyland kept referencing a 'final plan' in case Dominion City became compromised. He said they'd need to start again elsewhere, to rebuild. He called it a 'Rebirth.'"

Max clenched his fists, anger flaring up as he realized the full extent of the Sovereigns' foresight. Even as their organization crumbled in Dominion City, they'd prepared for the possibility, devising a plan to pick up the pieces and re-establish their power in another city, another state. They were more than just a cult—they were a calculated force, deeply entrenched and difficult to dismantle.

The chief entered the room, looking between them. "I've authorized teams to search those safehouses, but Reyland's influence runs deep. If he's slipped into hiding, we'll need more support than just our officers."

Max nodded. "We'll bring in the FBI. They need to know that this isn't just Dominion City's problem anymore. The Sovereigns are bigger than we thought."

The chief paused, taking in the grim reality of what they faced. "Do you think Reyland and his people could escape for good?"

Adrian's gaze hardened. "Not if we stay one step ahead. They're on the move, but they've left enough clues behind that we can trace them. And if they're carrying out this so-called 'Rebirth,' they'll need resources. They'll leave a trail."

Max looked at his team, determination clear in his eyes. "We've exposed them here, but we're far from finished. Reyland and his circle think they can start over, but we're not letting that happen. We'll track down every last one of them."

The chief nodded in agreement; his own expression resolute. "Then we make this a national investigation. We won't let them hide behind money and power anymore."

Back in the Precinct's War Room, as the operation to locate and apprehend Reyland and the other Sovereigns kicked into high gear, Max, Adrian, Sarah, and Emily returned to the precinct's war room, where they coordinated their efforts with other precincts and FBI representatives. Maps with pinned locations and names of suspects still at large filled the walls, creating a grim mosaic of the Sovereigns' extensive reach.

Sarah leaned over a map, tracing lines between different cities where Sovereign contacts were rumored to be hiding. "If we focus on intercepting their travel routes, we might have a chance to corner them. Reyland and the others know how to evade, but if they're still coordinating, they'll need communication channels, banks, logistics."

Emily added, "And if they're moving toward 'The Legacy' vault, they'll have a secure way of reaching it, somewhere isolated but well-defended."

Adrian exhaled, the enormity of the task ahead sinking in. "It's going to take everything we've got. If the Sovereigns have spread this far, we're talking about an investigation that might stretch for years."

Max placed a hand on Adrian's shoulder, his gaze steady. "Then we commit to it. Until every one of them is found."

The room fell silent, each of them taking in the long road ahead. This fight would be more than just a series of arrests; it would require relentless pursuit, alliances with law enforcement across the country, and unwavering dedication to rooting out the Sovereigns' influence wherever it lingered.

But there was something else in the silence—a sense of resolve, a shared understanding that Dominion City's ordeal had awakened them all to a purpose greater than they'd known before. The Sovereigns had thrived on secrecy, manipulation, and fear. But now, with their veil lifted, Max, Adrian, Sarah, and Emily had found something far more powerful: the truth.

The chief addressed them all, his voice firm. "You've all done incredible work. This isn't just about Dominion City anymore—it's about ensuring that no city, no town, is ever manipulated by this kind of force again. It's going to take time, but this is the beginning of the end for the Sovereigns."

Max nodded, a quiet but fierce determination filling his gaze. "We'll find them, no matter where they run. They've hidden in the shadows long enough."

And as the night deepened over Dominion City, Max and his team braced themselves for the journey ahead, ready to hunt down every last remnant of the Sovereigns,

The precinct was silent and dim, the last traces of sunlight disappearing over the city as Max sat alone in his office. Papers were scattered across his desk—photos, notes, and files from the Sovereigns' case. He leaned back in his chair, his eyes tired but unyielding, as he stared at a single sheet of paper pinned to the wall: a list of names, each one connected to the cult's vast network.

This investigation had been more than a case. For Max, it had been a journey of loss, vengeance, and ultimately, closure. He ran his fingers over the edge of his desk, his thoughts drifting to his late wife, Lauren, whose murder had set him on a path he could never have anticipated. The truth had been agonizing—knowing she'd been silenced by the very cult whose power he was only now dismantling. But he'd honored her memory. He'd finished the work she had started, and while it didn't bring her back, it gave him a sense of purpose he hadn't felt in years.

The faint rustle of footsteps broke the quiet. Adrian appeared in the doorway, carrying two cups of coffee, a silent invitation for a shared moment. Max gave a small nod, and Adrian stepped in, taking the chair across from him.

"You look like you could use this," Adrian said, sliding one of the cups across the desk. "Figured we both could."

Max accepted the coffee, the warmth seeping into his hands as he held the cup. They sat in silence, each reflecting on the chaos of the past weeks, the revelation of betrayals, the cracks in Dominion City's façade, and the cult that had nearly consumed them both.

After a long pause, Max broke the silence, his voice steady. "I thought taking down the Sovereigns would feel like a victory. But with Reyland still out there, with so many pieces still missing... it feels unfinished."

Adrian nodded, understanding. "I feel it too. We've exposed them, but they're still out there, and we know they're regrouping. It's not over."

Max set his cup down, a flicker of determination in his gaze. "It won't be over until they're all brought to justice, every last one of them. I'm not stopping until I know Dominion City is safe—and that no one else loses their family to their power."

Adrian's expression softened, a note of respect in his gaze. "You know, Max... I don't think I've ever really understood what drove you. But now? I think I get it. This case, it's about more than just the Sovereigns. It's about fighting for the people they hurt. The ones like... like your wife, and all those who've been silenced."

Max felt a lump form in his throat, but he managed a nod. "Lauren spent years investigating corruption in this city. She knew the risks, but she believed that if she exposed the truth, things would change. They killed her for that belief, and for a long time, I thought I'd never get justice for her."

He paused, his gaze turning distant. "But now I have the chance to finish what she started. To make sure her sacrifice wasn't in vain."

Adrian placed his coffee on the desk, leaning forward. "Then we do this together. We chase every lead, follow every trail, and find every last one of them. You have my word, Max. This fight isn't just yours anymore—it's ours."

Max nodded, his respect for Adrian deepening. They'd started as rivals, each driven by pride and competition, but now they stood united by something stronger—a shared commitment to justice and a determination to protect their city from the darkness that had threatened to consume it.

A quiet knock sounded at the door, and Sarah stepped in, a file tucked under her arm. "I thought you might want to see this," she said, placing the folder on Max's desk. "These are the latest intel reports from the FBI. They've flagged a few of Reyland's known associates as suspects who might be helping him hide."

Max opened the file, scanning the names and locations. Each line seemed to carry a sense of urgency, a reminder that the Sovereigns' reach still extended beyond Dominion City. He looked up at Sarah, gratitude evident in his eyes.

"Thank you, Sarah," he said. "I know this hasn't been easy for you either."

Sarah's expression was resolute. "This city deserves the truth. And after everything we've seen, I'm not stopping until every last piece of this story is told."

Emily stepped into the doorway, listening quietly, her presence a reminder of the lives touched by the Sovereigns. She looked at Max, her voice filled with quiet resolve. "I'll be helping too. They took so much from me, from my father... but I'm not afraid of them anymore. Whatever you need, I'll be there."

Max felt a renewed strength as he looked at his team. They were bruised, battle-worn, but together, they'd become a force the Sovereigns couldn't control.

As he looked back at the folder on his desk, his mind racing with the task ahead, Max felt something he hadn't allowed himself to feel in a long time: hope.

He stood, gathering the files and maps, his shoulders set with determination. "We're not just dismantling a cult," he said. "We're rebuilding this city. We're making it safe again."

Adrian nodded; his eyes filled with the same determination. "Then let's get started. Because I have a feeling Reyland isn't going to stay hidden for long."

The group exchanged a silent agreement, each of them aware of the challenges that lay ahead, but ready to face them together.

Max returned home late that night; the city quiet as he opened the door to his apartment. Stacks of case files filled his living room, remnants of every investigation he'd pursued, every lead he'd followed in his years as a detective. But his eyes lingered on a single, small box tucked away on a shelf—the last belongings of his wife, Lauren.

He walked over, opening the box slowly. Inside were her journal, her press pass, and a small, worn notebook where she'd scribbled her notes, piecing together the puzzle of corruption she'd uncovered years ago. Her words, scrawled in her familiar handwriting, felt like a message, a final connection between them.

Max closed the notebook, holding it in his hands as he looked out the window, his gaze fixed on the city skyline. "I'll finish this, Lauren," he murmured softly. "I'll make sure they never hurt anyone again."

He took a deep breath, feeling the weight of his promise settle over him. The Sovereigns had been powerful, ruthless, and cunning. They'd taken his wife, torn families apart, and wielded their influence to control a city. But their power was weakening, their secrets exposed, and for the first time, Dominion City was beginning to see the light.

As dawn broke over the city, Max felt a renewed sense of purpose. The Sovereigns weren't gone yet, but he would hunt down every last one of them. He would ensure their influence died with them, and that the city they'd held in a chokehold would finally be free.

The sun was just beginning to rise over Dominion City, casting a soft, golden light across the buildings as the city slowly came to life. Max walked through the streets, the echoes of last night's protests still resonating in his mind. The people's voices had been loud and fierce, their anger and heartbreak a palpable force as they demanded justice, transparency, and an end to the corruption that had stained their home.

Max passed a small café where the owner had propped open the door to let in the morning air. A local radio station played in the background, the announcer's voice reflecting the city's tense atmosphere.

"After the revelation of the Sovereigns' extensive influence over our city, Dominion faces a crossroads. Leaders have promised swift action and sweeping reforms, but many citizens wonder… will it be enough?"

Max paused, glancing into the café where a few patrons sat, their faces a mixture of hope and uncertainty. He understood their skepticism. The Sovereigns' exposure was a monumental victory, but the fight wasn't over. People like Reyland were still out there, hiding in the shadows, waiting for the storm to pass. For them, Dominion City wasn't just a place; it was an empire, and they would do anything to take it back.

The thought sent a familiar chill down his spine, but he felt a quiet determination take its place. He was done running from the darkness. Now, he was part of the light that would chase it down.

As he continued through the square, he caught sight of Sarah and Emily setting up for a live broadcast. Emily's shoulders were square, her face calm but resolute as she adjusted her microphone.

She'd come a long way, finding strength in her vulnerability, and now, she was ready to tell the city her story. Sarah gave him a nod of acknowledgment, a silent promise that she'd continue to dig, to expose every last remnant of the Sovereigns' influence.

Max felt a surge of pride as he watched them. They were survivors, and together, they would ensure the city stayed vigilant.

As he made his way toward the precinct, he noticed something that made him pause. Across the street, a man in a long coat stood with his back to him, looking up at one of the buildings. Something about the man's stance seemed oddly familiar. Then he saw it—a glint of silver dangling from the man's wrist, a bracelet engraved with a symbol that sent a shock through Max's system: three interlocking circles.

The Sovereigns' emblem.

Max's heart raced, but he remained calm, keeping the man in his periphery as he continued his walk. Whoever this man was, he'd clearly been sent as a message—a reminder that even though Dominion City's cult had been exposed, its followers weren't giving up.

The man glanced over his shoulder, his eyes briefly meeting Max's. There was no hint of fear in his expression, just a knowing look, a subtle acknowledgment that he understood the game was far from over. He turned and slipped into the crowd, disappearing down a side street, but the unspoken message lingered in Max's mind.

The Sovereigns had weakened, but they weren't defeated.

Max felt the familiar resolve harden in his chest. This wasn't a victory lap—it was only the beginning. He knew there would be others like Reyland, others who would try to claw back the power they had lost. But now, Max and his team had something they hadn't had before: the people's trust, and a commitment to keeping the truth in the open.

As he reached the precinct, Adrian met him at the entrance, his face serious. "Got your message," Adrian said, nodding toward where the man had been standing. "Looks like they're testing us already."

Max managed a wry smile. "Let them. The Sovereigns think they can hide in plain sight, wait until things cool down. But we're not going to give them the chance."

Adrian's expression mirrored his own determination. "You know, a few months ago, I would have thought we'd be celebrating right now. But it feels like we're just getting started."

Max nodded. "Because we are. There are people in this city who still need justice, families who lost loved ones, lives that were destroyed by this cult. And now, we have a duty to make sure they're all held accountable."

They entered the precinct together, walking down the familiar corridors lined with bulletin boards filled with news clippings and case files. A sense of quiet purpose settled over them both. Their work was no longer just about revenge or redemption—it was about rebuilding a city that had been fractured, creating a place where truth and accountability could thrive.

As they reached the war room, Max noticed the list of names on the wall—key members of the Sovereigns who were still unaccounted for. Reyland's name was circled in red, a reminder that their mission was still incomplete.

He turned to Adrian. "We're going to track down every lead, follow every rumor, and we won't stop until every last one of them is found."

Adrian nodded, his gaze never wavering. "Then let's get to work."

Later in the day, the city square was filled with people gathering for a vigil, a symbol of unity in the face of the tragedy and betrayal Dominion City had endured. Max stood at the edge of the crowd, his hands in his pockets, watching as citizens lit candles, each one representing a life touched by the Sovereigns' actions. Faces reflected the glow of the candles—some angry, others grieving, but many filled with resilience.

Max spotted Emily, who was speaking to a small group of people, her voice strong as she shared her story, refusing to let her fear silence her any longer. Nearby, Sarah recorded her speech, capturing the moment for her next article, her notepad and recorder ready to document the ongoing journey.

Max felt a deep sense of respect as he watched them, realizing that their stories were now woven into the city's fabric, symbols of the city's strength and survival. Dominion City had been scarred, yes, but it had not been broken.

He stepped back, letting the crowd absorb him as he walked through the square, his steps purposeful, his gaze scanning the streets that he knew so well. There would always be shadows in this city, remnants of the cult and its followers who would try to reclaim their hold. But Max knew now that he wasn't alone in the fight.

As he moved through the crowd, a young woman approached him, her face illuminated by candlelight. She looked at him with a mixture of gratitude and determination. "Thank you, Detective Carter. For fighting for us, for the truth."

Max gave her a slight nod, humbled. "I'm just doing my job. The real strength... it comes from all of you."

She smiled, the light of the candle flickering between them. "Well, we'll keep fighting, too. We'll be watching."

As she walked away, Max felt a renewed sense of purpose. Dominion City had woken up, and with its people on guard, the Sovereigns wouldn't find it so easy to creep back into power.

The city was still healing, still vulnerable, but it was no longer defenseless. And as long as Max had breath in his body, he'd continue the work he'd begun, standing as a protector, a guardian, against those who sought to plunge Dominion back into darkness.

As the sun set, casting a warm glow over the square, Max looked out over the city, his city. He was ready for whatever lay ahead, knowing that the fight for Dominion's soul was ongoing—and that he'd be there, watchful and unyielding, until the last shadow was driven away.

Milton Keynes UK
Ingram Content Group UK Ltd.
UKHW031047291124
451807UK00001B/64